Joh

Questions for Written Examination

Anatiposi

John Swett

Questions for Written Examination

Reprint of the original, first published in 1872.

1st Edition 2023 | ISBN: 978-3-38213-322-1

Anatiposi Verlag is an imprint of Outlook Verlagsgesellschaft mbH.

Verlag (Publisher): Outlook Verlag GmbH, Zeilweg 44, 60439 Frankfurt, Deutschland
Vertretungsberechtigt (Authorized to represent): E. Roepke, Zeilweg 44, 60439 Frankfurt, Deutschland
Druck (Print): Books on Demand GmbH, In de Tarpen 42, 22848 Norderstedt, Deutschland

QUESTIONS

FOR

WRITTEN EXAMINATIONS:

AN AID TO

CANDIDATES FOR TEACHERS' CERTIFICATES,

AND

A HAND-BOOK

FOR EXAMINERS AND TEACHERS.

BY

JOHN SWETT,

LATE SUPERINTENDENT OF PUBLIC INSTRUCTION OF CALIFORNIA.

NEW YORK:

IVISON, BLAKEMAN, TAYLOR, AND COMPANY.

RIVERSIDE, CAMBRIDGE:
STEREOTYPED AND PRINTED BY
H. O. HOUGHTON AND COMPANY.

PREFACE.

In many States and cities the examination of applicants for certificates to teach in the public schools is conducted in writing.

In many cities the promotion of pupils from one grade to another is determined by means of written examinations.

Any one who has had occasion to prepare many sets of examination questions is well aware that it requires time, study, care, and good judgment to devise queries which shall be a fair test of the knowledge of the pupils or teachers to be examined.

The sets of questions in this compilation have all been used in actual examinations of schools and of teachers. Those by the present writer will be found marked "S." The others have been drawn from the various sets used in Chicago, Cincinnati, St. Louis, Providence, San Francisco, and other cities.

They present a fair average of the general test to which teachers and pupils are subjected.

They will be found useful to teachers who are preparing for examination, because a study of them will secure the main points in the important studies.

They will be useful to examiners, because they are suggestive of principles.

They will be useful to inexperienced teachers in examining their own classes.

They will be convenient for the use of principals of schools who cannot find time to prepare varied sets of questions for monthly or annual examinations.

Finally, it may be remarked that the mind of any one teacher is apt to run in certain *grooves:* hence questions prepared by some one else are likely to prove valuable and suggestive to even the best teacher.

The Hand-Book is divided into two Parts — Part I. being sets of questions used in the examination of teachers, containing 100 sets and 1,000 questions; and Part II being papers used in written examinations for grammar schools, containing 100 sets and 1,200 questions.

CONTENTS.

PART I.

SETS OF QUESTIONS USED IN THE EXAMINATION OF TEACHERS.

PART II.

WRITTEN EXAMINATION FOR GRAMMAR SCHOOLS.

PART I.

SETS OF QUESTIONS

USED IN THE

EXAMINATION OF TEACHERS.

CONTAINING ONE HUNDRED SETS AND ONE THOUSAND QUESTIONS.

EXAMINATION RULES AND DIRECTIONS

1. On the blank side of each of the cards given to you, write your name in full, keep one card to enable you to remember your number in the examination, and return the other to the examiners.

2. Write your *number* — not your name — and the name of the study for which the answers are made, on each paper.

3. Write on one side only of each half-sheet and number the written pages.

4. Divide your answers into paragraphs, and write in a legible hand.

5. No communication, either by signs or by whispering, will be allowed. The papers of any persons so offending will be thrown out of the examination.

6. No reference to books allowed during time of examination.

7. No persons absent during the examination in any one study, will be allowed to pass examination in that study, unless they were necessarily absent on account of sickness.

8. If you find questions which you cannot answer, pass them, and answer such as you can.

9. Number all answers to correspond with the questions and sub-divisions of questions.

10. Make your answers clear, definite, and complete.

11. If you do not understand the meaning of a question, signify it by raising your hand.

12. Read each set of questions through before you begin your work.

13. After you have completed a paper, examine it carefully with reference to spelling, capitals, and punctuation. S.

ARITHMETIC.

SET I.

TOTAL: FIFTEEN QUESTIONS — ONE HUNDRED CREDITS.

Ten Questions — Five Credits Each.

1. How many times must 25 be added to itself to make 625? Explain.

2. Divide $\frac{1}{4}$ by $\frac{2}{3}$ and give some kind of analytical reason, showing *how* you obtain the result, and *why*? (The common rule of inverting, etc., will not be taken as a sufficient answer.)

3. Divide the decimal .337 by 2, explain each step in the division, and show *why* you point off as you do.

4. Multiply .25 by the decimal five hundredths; explain each step and show *why* you point off as you do.

5. Divide $7.00 by half a cent. Multiply $5.00 by $5.00.

6. Divide 17 miles, 15 rods, 2 yards, 2 feet, 5 inches by 3.

7. Interest of $150 from December 30th, 1870, to November 16th, 1871, at 10 per cent. a year.

8. Add $\frac{7}{12}$, $\frac{7}{15}$, and the decimals .125 and .45.

9. Compound interest of $100 at 2 per cent. a month, compounded monthly for 10 months.

10. Bank discount of $400 for 6 months at $1\frac{1}{4}$ per cent. a month.

Five Questions — Ten Credits Each.

11. What per cent. of ½ is ⅓?

12. A boy bought pencils at the rate of 5 for 4 cents, and sold them at the rate of 4 for 5 cents; what per cent. did he gain?

13. A room in the shape of a perfect cube contains 15,625 cubic feet; how far is it from one corner on the floor to the corner diagonally opposite on the ceiling?

14. A teacher contracted to teach school for 10 months at $100 a month, to be paid at the end of each month. The trustees having no money, nothing was paid her until the end of the 10 months, when the trustees allowed her interest at the rate of 12 per cent. a year. What was the amount of her wages?

15. Mary Brown borrowed of Sarah Smith $400 in gold coin, on the 10th of June, 1869. On the 20th of July, 1870, $200 was paid on the note. What was due December 1st, 1870? Rate of interest 10 per cent. a year. Write a note and put the indorsement on the back. S.

SET II.

TEN QUESTIONS — TEN CREDITS EACH.

1. Change ⅝ to a decimal, multiply by four thousandths, divide the product by five millionths, and add five hundredths.

2. Find the sum, difference, and product of ⅞ and ⅔.

3. What decimal part of £1 is 9*s.* 2*d.* 1.12 *far.*?

4. Find the greatest common divisor and least common multiple of 18, 24, 30, 36.

5. A merchant sold sugar at 8 cents a pound, and gained 10 per cent.; what per cent. would he have gained had he sold it at 9 cents a pound?

6. What is the bank discount on $200 for 60 days, at $1\frac{3}{4}$ per cent. per month?

7. What is the interest on a promissory note of $450, from January 3d, 1863, to May 7th, 1863, at $2\frac{1}{2}$ per cent. a month?

8. Write a promissory note, drawn by John Doe in favor of Richard Roe, for $500, payable on demand, with interest at 10 per cent. per annum, dated January 12th, 1861. Write on this note, in due form, the following indorsements:—

June 5th, 1862. Received $150.
May 4th, 1863. Received $200.

What is due on this note, May 9th, 1863?

9. In a geometrical progression, the first term is 64, the ratio $\frac{1}{2}$; what is the tenth term?

10. What is the cube root of 67917312?

SET III.

TOTAL: FIFTEEN QUESTIONS — ONE HUNDRED CREDITS.

Ten Questions — Five Credits Each.

1. Multiply 67899 by 9999. From thirty millions thirty thousand and thirty, take three millions three thousand and three.

2. When it is noon at London, what will be the time at the mouth of the Columbia River, which is 120 degrees west of London?

3. $52\frac{1}{2}$ by $7\frac{1}{5}$: subtract $14\frac{2}{3}$ from the product, and divide the remainder by $\frac{7}{8}$.

4. What number is that which being increased by $\frac{2}{3}$ of $\frac{3}{5}$ of $10\frac{5}{7}$, and the sum diminished by $7\frac{1}{2}$, will give a remainder of $9\frac{3}{7}$?

5. Divide seventy-seven millionths by seventy-seven ten thousandths. Divide one mill by one dollar.

6. Name all the coins issued from the United States Mint, and give the sum of the values of one of each kind.

7. Paid $8 a pair for a case of boots: how shall I mark the same so that I may fall 12 per cent. from the marked price, and yet make 10 per cent. on the cost?

8. A merchant sold $1,500 worth of goods, one half to be paid in 6 months, the other half in 9 months; what sum must be received for them in cash after deducting interest at the rate of 2 per cent. a month?

9. Sold 5,000 pounds of sugar at 9 cents a pound, and lost 10 per cent.; what per cent. should I gain by selling at 12 cents a pound?

10. A room is 25 feet long, 20 feet wide, and 12 feet high: how far from one lower corner to the opposite upper corner? S.

Five Questions — Ten Credits Each.

11. A ladder 40 feet long will reach a window 32 feet high on one side of a street, and on the other side another window 24 feet high? What is the breadth of the street?

12. A note for $280 bears date January 1st, 1863, and is given for 2 years, 7 months, 6 days, at 10 per cent. per annum. Upon this note there is a payment indorsed January 1st, 1864, of $75; what is due upon the note at its maturity?

13. A room is 20 feet long, 18 feet wide, and 12 feet high; how many yards of carpeting, $\frac{3}{4}$ of a yard wide, will it take to carpet the floor, and how many yards of paper, $\frac{5}{8}$ of a yard wide, will be required to paper the four walls, deducting 30 square feet for windows?

14 What is the square of $\frac{2}{3}$? Of .25? Square root of $\frac{1.6}{6.25}$? Of 1?

15. What is the bank discount, and what the inter on $2,500 for 90 days, at 10 per cent. a year?

SET IV.

TOTAL: SEVENTEEN QUESTIONS — ONE HUNDRED CREDITS.

Ten Questions — Five Credits Each.

1. In addition, after adding a column, why do you carry the left hand figure and write the right hand figure?

2. Divide 375 by 2, and explain why you suppose the remainder of each separate figure, after division, to be placed before the next succeeding figure.

3. How may times can 144 be subtracted from 1728?

4. What will $5\frac{1}{2}$ miles of telegraph wire cost at 7 cents a foot.

5. How many cubic feet is a room 14.5 feet long, 12.05 feet wide, and 10.1 feet high? How many yards of carpet will cover the floor?

6. Divide 10 by $\frac{2}{3}$ and explain *why* you perform it as you do. (No credits allowed unless an analytical reason be given. The solution by *rule* only will be allowed nothing.)

7. Multiply the decimal twelve ten thousandths by the decimal twelve thousandths, and divide the product by the decimal six hundredths.

8. Divide the decimal .024 by the common fraction $\frac{1}{3}$.

9. Divide 7 months, 1 week, 3 days, 5 minutes, 9 seconds by 2.

10. Divide $4.00 by one fourth of a cent. S.

Five Questions — Ten Credits Each.

11. You sell to Mrs. Richard Roe, 12½ yards of calico at 12½ cents a yard, 3¼ yards of silk at $4.50 a yard, 11½ yards of ribbon at 25 cents a yard, and 25½ yards of cotton cloth at 20 cents a yard. Make out your bill.

12. 3 is what per cent. of 9.

13. You hire of John Smith, $100 in gold, for six months, at the rate of 10 per cent. a year. Write a note for it.

14. What is 12½ per cent. of 18,776 lbs. of wheat, and what will it cost at 1½ cents a lb.?

15. Interest of $75 from January 12th, 1871, to December 11th, 1871, at 1¼ per cent. a month?

16. Extract the square root of 2209.

17. A degree is 69½ miles; how many inches in the circumference of the earth?

SET V.

TEN QUESTIONS — TEN CREDITS EACH.

1. Resolve 18, 30, 36, 42, and 54 into their prime factors, and select the factors which produce the greatest common divisor, and explain the reason of the selection.

2. If $\frac{2}{3}$ of $\frac{4}{5}$ of $3\frac{1}{2}$ times any number be multiplied by $\frac{3}{4}$, the product divided by $\frac{2}{5}$, the quotient increased by $4\frac{1}{6}$. and the sum diminished by $\frac{1}{5}$ of itself, the remainder will be how many times the number?

3. Divide $\dfrac{\frac{1}{3} \text{ of } (\frac{2}{3})^3 \times 3\frac{1}{4}}{\frac{1}{2} \text{ of } (9\frac{1}{4})^2 \times (\frac{2}{3})^4}$ by the square root of $\dfrac{\frac{3}{4} \text{ of } 5\frac{1}{3}}{(\frac{1}{2})^3 \text{ of } 8}$.

4. A man invests $5,000 in foreign goods when gold is $1.12; what must he sell the goods for in

currency in order to make 25 per cent. on the gold investment ?

5. What must I pay for government six per cents. that my investment may yield 9 per cent. in currency gold being at present rates ?

6. What must be the dimensions, in feet, of a bin, whose width and height are to be equal and half its length, to contain 1,000 bushels of corn ?

7. How many cubic inches of iron will be required to make 1,000 12-inch solid shot ?

8. In a given month 5 inches of rain fell ; what must be the height of a cistern whose diameter is to be 10 feet to hold the water which falls on the roof of a house 40 feet long by 20 feet wide, the ridge being 8 feet above the beam ?

9. If $\frac{2}{3}$ of A's money equals $\frac{3}{4}$ of B's, and $\frac{2}{3}$ of B's equals $\frac{3}{5}$ of C's, and the interest of all their money for 4 years and 8 months at 6 per cent. is $15,190, how much money has each ?

10. A can do a piece of work in 3 weeks ; B can do 4 times as much in 8 weeks ; and C can do 6 times as much in 14 weeks ; in what time can they all together do B's work ?

SET VI.

FIFTEEN QUESTIONS — FIVE CREDITS EACH.

1. Sold 5,520 bushels of grain, and lost 8 per cent.; how much per cent. would have been gained had it been sold at 60 cents per bushel ?

2. If 5 compositors, in 16 days, working 14 hours a day, can compose 20 sheets of 24 pages each, 50 lines on a page, and 40 letters in a line, in how many days, by working 7 hours a day. can 10 compositors compose 40 sheets of 16 pages each, 60 lines on a page, and 50 letters in a line ? Solve by proportion.

3. Suppose that a note for $1,413.72 is discounted at a bank at 1 per cent. a month for 6 months, how much money would be received from the bank for the note?

4. What is the difference between the interest and discount of $5,900 for 1 year and 6 months at 12 per cent. per annum?

5. A man purchased a farm for $3,600, and agrees to pay $600 down and the balance in 5 equal semi-annual installments; at what time may the whole be paid at once?

6. A man owns a farm in the form of a square, containing 250 acres; what is the length of the diagonal of the square?

7. When it is 12 M. in San Francisco, what time is it in Hong Kong, considering the latter city to be 240° east of the former?

8. It is 16 minutes of 2 o'clock P. M. at the City of Mexico when it is 12 M. at San Francisco. What is the longitude of the City of Mexico?

9. A, of San Francisco, remits $12,960 to B, of New York, directing him to invest in sugar what remains after he (B) has deducted his commission at 8 per cent. If B pays 8¼ cents a pound for the sugar, how many pounds will he purchase, and what will be his commission?

10. A merchant sells ⅝ of a lot of goods for what the whole cost. What does he gain per cent.?

11. Which is the heavier, a pound of silver or a pound of cotton?

12. What is the square root of the cube of 24?

13. Give the analysis of the process of dividing one fraction by another.

14. Write the form of a promissory note for $6,000.

15. What is the square root of the square of $\frac{3}{25}$ of the square of $\frac{12}{125}$.

SET VII.

TEN QUESTIONS — TEN CREDITS EACH.

1. Find the sum of the following decimals: 20020 millionths; 50005 thousandths; one million ten-thousandths; 3207½ tenths; eighty thousand hundredths.

2. What is the smallest sum of money with which you could buy postage stamps at 10, 12, 15, 24, and 90 cents each, expending the whole sum?

3. Write a promissory note for $250 due in 8 months, at 8 per cent., and find the amount to be paid at the time of settlement.

4. A and B were in business together for 3 years, and gained $4,800. A put in at first $2,000, and at the end of 1 year $1,500 more. B put in at first $1,500, and at the end of 2 years $2,500 more. Required the gain of each.

5. Supply the terms 6 :   :: 9 : 30.
12 : 40 ::   : 60.

6. On a note for $3,500 at 7 per cent. there is interest due for 1 year and 6 months. How much gold at a premium of 34 per cent. will be required to discharge the note?

7. Mr. Snow bought 1 acre of land which bordered on the street 100 feet. How far back did it extend, the lot being rectangular?

8. James and John together have $5,893, but James has $125 more than 3 times as much as John. How much has each?

9. A, B, and C found $96, which they agree to share in the proportions of the numbers 3, 4, and 5. How much should each have?

10. A pole 63 feet long was broken into 2 pieces, the shorter being $\frac{2}{5}$ of the longer. Required the length of each piece.

SET VIII.

TEN QUESTIONS—TEN CREDITS EACH.

1. What is the interest on $850, from January 19th to May 11th, 1864, at $1\frac{3}{4}$ per cent. a month, interest payable monthly and compounded.

2. What is the present worth of a note for $500, due in $2\frac{1}{2}$ months, at 2 per cent. a month? What the discount?

3. In how many different orders may 10 school-boys seat themselves on a recitation bench?

4. Multiply .0125 by .999, and divide the product by .25.

5. Extract the cube root of 830584.

6. If a grocer sells sugar at 10 cents a pound, and gains 10 per cent. on the cost, what per cent. will he gain by selling at 11 cents a pound?

7. What is the 10th term of the series of which 1 is the first term and $\frac{1}{2}$ the common ratio.

8. How many pounds of iron are equal in weight to 100 pounds of gold.

9. A certain room is 16 feet wide, 20 feet long, and 12 feet high. What is the distance from the right-hand upper corner to the left-hand lower corner?

10. What part of one mile is 7 furlongs, 4 rods, 2 yards, 1 foot, 4 inches. S.

SET IX.

LOWEST GRADE, OR PRIMARY CERTIFICATES.

Note. — The following sets of Arithmetic questions, from IX. to XIII. inclusive, represent the average standard for certificates for teaching in Primary Schools.

1. Multiply 3.56 by .048 and divide the product by 48.

2. $346\frac{5}{8} + \frac{9}{20} + \frac{3}{4}$ of $\frac{8}{9} + 49\frac{5}{6} =$ what?

3. Multiply $15\frac{3}{4}$ by $\frac{4}{21}$ and divide the product by 27.

4. A, B, and C can do a piece of work in 5 days; B and C can do it in 8 days; in what time can A do it?

5. If 5 be added to both terms of the fraction $\frac{7}{8}$, will its value be increased or diminished, and how much?

6. If $\$7\frac{1}{4}$ will buy $3\frac{1}{4}$ cords of wood, how many cords of wood can be bought for $\$10\frac{1}{2}$?

7. Add $\frac{2}{3}$ of a mile, $\frac{1}{2}$ of a furlong, and $\frac{3}{18}$ of a rod together.

8. On the 8th of May, 1868, William Darrow borrowed of Howard Barlow $356.25, and agreed to pay him in 7 months, with interest at $1\frac{1}{4}$ per cent. per month. Make out the proper note and find the interest accrued at maturity.

9. Bought clover seed at 50 cents a pound, and sold it for $57\frac{1}{2}$ cents. What per cent. was gained?

10. A room is 18 feet long and 14 feet wide; how many yards of carpet 30 inches wide will it take to cover it? S.

SET X.

1. Write the prime numbers from 1 to 47.

2. Solve, by cancellation, $\frac{49 \times 33 \times 94 \times 5 \times 13}{65 \times 47 \times 77 \times 21}$.

3. Find the greatest common divisor of 252, 630, 1134, and 1386.

4. What is the least common multiple of 1, 2, 3, 4, 5, 6, 7, 8, 9?

5. Reduce $\frac{5643}{5940}$ to its lowest terms.

6. A man, having \$$25\frac{7}{8}$, paid \$$6\frac{1}{2}$ for coal, \$$2\frac{1}{5}$ for dry goods, and \$$\frac{3}{4}$ for a pound of tea; how much had he left?

7. How many tons of hay can be purchased for \$$119\frac{7}{16}$ at \$$9\frac{3}{8}$ per ton?

8. A certain sum of money is to be divided among 5 persons: A is to have $\frac{1}{4}$, B $\frac{1}{5}$, C $\frac{1}{10}$, D $\frac{1}{25}$, and E the remainder, which is \$$20\frac{1}{2}$; what is the whole sum to be divided?

9. What part of 9 feet square are 9 square feet?

10. How many square feet of boards in a tight fence surrounding a field 1 mile square, the fence being 5 feet high?

SET XI.

1. Divide 409887 by 47, and multiply the quotient by 246.

2. Find the prime factor of 798.

3. What is the greatest common divisor of 484391 and 684877?

4. Add $\frac{3}{5}$, $\frac{4}{7}$, $\frac{13}{21}$, $\frac{7}{15}$, and from the sum subtract $1\frac{1}{2}$.

5. Multiply $2\frac{1}{3}$ by $1\frac{4}{5}$, and divide the product by 4^1.

6. Change $\frac{3}{4}$ to a decimal fraction, multiply by .0008, and divide the product by .02.

7. Change $\frac{5}{8}$ of a ton to integers of a lower denomination.

8. Change .645 of a day to integers of a lower denomination.

9. What is the interest on \$1,200 from June 15th, 1862, to May 4th, 1863, at 6 per cent. per annum?

10. What is the bank discount on $400 for 60 days, at 2 per cent. a month? S.

SET XII.

1. Change five eighths to a decimal, multiply by four thousandths, and divide the product by five millionths.

2. Find the sum, difference, product, and quotient of $\frac{7}{8}$ and $\frac{2}{3}$.

3. Find the greatest common divisor and the least common multiple of 18, 24, 30, 36.

4. What decimal part of £1 is 19*s.* 2*d.* 2.12 *far.*?

5. Divide two mills by ten dollars, and multiply one hundred dollars by the quotient.

6. Divide 3 miles, 75 rods, 9 feet, 11 inches, by 2, and from the quotient subtract 75 yards.

7. What is the interest on a note of $800 from January 1st, 1872, to March 4th, 1872, at $1\frac{1}{2}$ per cent. a month, compounded monthly?

8. A grocer sold raisins at 22 cents per pound and gained 10 per cent.; what per cent. would he have gained had he sold them at 24 cents per pound?

9. What is the square root of 39.0625?

10. A boy bought apples at the rate of 3 for 2 cents, and sold them at the rate of 2 for 3 cents; what per cent. did he make? S.

SET XIII.

TOTAL: FIFTEEN QUESTIONS — ONE HUNDRED CREDITS.

Ten Questions — Five Credits Each.

1. Express 90275 by the Roman method of notation.

2. Multiply 475286 by 9999.

3. Multiply 45625 by 25, and divide the product by 99.

4. Multiply £5 8*s.* 5*d.* 3 *fars.* by 7, and divide the product by 3.

5. Change £5 8*s.* 5*d.* 3 *qrs.* to pounds, and the decimal of a pound.

6. How many three cent pieces are there in a double eagle?

7. Which is heavier, a pound of gold or a pound of iron? an ounce of silver or an ounce of lead?

8. What part of 4 feet square is 4 square feet?

9. Multiply the decimal 2.75 by 1.2, and divide the product by .0011.

10. Change $\frac{5}{8}$ to a decimal fraction.

Five Questions — Ten Credits Each.

11. Find the greatest common divisor and the least common multiple of 18, 48, 72, 66.

12. Resolve 24736 into its prime factors.

13. 18 multiplied by $\frac{1}{2}$, divided by $\frac{1}{3}$, multiplied by $\frac{5}{7}$, divided by $\frac{3}{5}$, multiplied by 4, equals what?

14. $\frac{4}{5}$ divided by $\frac{2}{3}$, minus $\frac{3}{8}$, divided by $\frac{1}{3}$, minus $\frac{8}{10}$, equals what?

15. $\frac{5}{12}$ plus $\frac{7}{8}$ plus $\frac{9}{10}$ plus $\frac{3}{16}$ minus $\frac{3}{25}$ of $\frac{15}{27}$ equals what? S.

ENGLISH GRAMMAR.

SET I.

TOTAL: FOURTEEN QUESTIONS — ONE HUNDRED CREDITS.

Twelve Questions — Five Credits Each.

1. WRITE a complex sentence, and give a general analysis of it.

2. How are nouns varied to indicate number and gender?

3. What classes of words are used as connectives?

4. Write sentences to show the correct use of the verbs *lie, lay, sit* and *set* in the future perfect (second future) tense, indicative mode.

5. Write the plurals of *wife, wharf, lily, money handful, pailful, motto, turkey.*

6. Compare the following adjectives: *best, worst, holy, next, first, last, less, evil, blue, supreme.*

7. Principal parts of the following verbs: *burst, throw, dive, heat, drink, eat, build, strive, lay, lie.*

8. Synopsis of the verb *eat* in the third person singular, indicative mode, passive voice.

9. Correct the following sentences: —

I have less books than you.

She was more active but not so studious as Mary.

Who had I ought to have given this to?

I intended to have gone, but, between you and I, I am glad I didn't.

She looks sweetly and seems nicely.

10. Analyze the sentence, "Teach me what is right," and parse each word.

11. Decline *whom*, *which*, *it*, *her*, and *ye*.

12. When is the relative *that* used in preference to *who* or *which?* What is the difference in the use of *shall* and *will* to express future time?

Two Questions — Twenty Credits Each.

13. "Let not ambition mock their useful toil,
Their homely joys, and destiny obscure;
Nor grandeur hear with a disdainful smile
The short and simple annals of the poor."

GRAY'S *Elegy.*

(*a*). (Four Credits.) — What kind of a sentence is the preceding stanza?

(*b*). (Four Credits.) — Parse *mock.*

(*c*). (Four Credits.) — In what case is *grandeur?*

(*d*). (Four Credits.) — Parse *obscure.*

(*e*). (Four Credits.) — Parse *hear.*

14. Correct the spelling, punctuation, and errors of the following extract from Dickens: —

"None knew this better than the idlest boys who growing bolder with impunyty waxed louder and daringer playing odd or even under the masters' eye eating apples openly and without rebuke pinching each other in sport or malise without the least rezerve and cuting there inishials in the very legs of the desk."

(Ten credits for correct writing, and ten for the following questions:) —

(*a*) What kind of a sentence is this extract?

(*b*) In what case is *boys?*

(*c*) Parse *waxed.*

(*d*) Parse *initials.*

(*e*) Parse *better.*

S.

SET II.

1. (Two Credits.) — Write a sentence in which *laid* and *lain* are correctly used in the future perfect, or second future tense.

2. (Two Credits.) — What is meant by the person and number of verbs? Illustrate by an example.

3. (Two Credits.) — Plural of *staff, capful, beau, genus, crisis, vertebra, Miss Brown, Mr. Smith.*

4. (Two Credits.) — Principal parts of *let, bid, see, hide, sink, slay, bless, burn, burst, dig, hang, work.*

5. (Two Credits.) — Conjugate the verb *be* in the past tense, subjunctive mode, and in the future perfect tense, indicative mode.

6. (Two Credits.) — Correct the following sentences: —

His family are large yet he supports them. Every house was burned, and every man, woman, and child were killed.

7. (*a*) (Two Credits.) — Correct and punctuate the following stanza: —

"Spake full well in language quaint and olden
 One who dwelleth by the castled rhine.
When he called the flowers so blue and golden
 Stars that in earths firmament do shine." — BRYANT.

(*b*) (Two Credits.) — Express the same thoughts in prose.

(*c*) (Two Credits.) — What kind of a sentence is the whole stanza?

(*d*) (Two Credits.) — Conjugate *dwelleth*, and parse *one.*

8. (Eight Credits. Half Credit off for each uncorrected grammatical error, and each word wrongly spelled.) — Rewrite and correct the following paragraph from the Declaration of Independence: —

"When in the coarse of human evvents it becoms nessessary for one people to dissolves the pollittical bands whitch has conected them with another and to asume among the Powers of the Earth the sepperate and equall station too which the laws of Nature and natures god entitel them a desent respect to the oppinions of mankind requires that they should declair the causes whitch impels them to the sepperasion."

9. (Two Credits.) — What kind of a sentence is the preceding, and why?

10. (Two Credits.) — Simple subject and simple predicate.

11. (Two Credits.) — "That they should declare," etc., is what kind of a clause, and what does it modify?

12. (Two Credits.) — "When in the course," etc., what is it, and what does it modify?

13. (Two Credits.). — "To which . . . . entitles them," is what, and what does it modify?

14. (Two Credits.) — Name all the nouns and verbs in the whole paragraph.

. . . . . "When thoughts
Of the last bitter hour come like a blight
Over thy spirit, and sad images
Of the stern agony, and shroud, and pall,
And breathless darkness, and the narrow house,
Make thee to shudder and grow sick at heart —
Go forth under the open sky and list
To Nature's teachings, while from all around
Earth and her waters, and the depths of air,
Comes a still voice: Yet, a few days, and thee
The all-beholding sun shall see no more
In all his course." — *Thanatopsis*, BRYANT.

15. (Two Credits.) — What kind of a sentence is the preceding stanza?

(*b*) (Two Credits.) — Name the subject and predicate of the most important proposition.

(*c*) (Two Credits.) — Name the adjective phrases and tell what they modify.

(*d*) (Two Credits.) — Parse *go* and *list* in the seventh line.

Note. — Use abbreviated models in parsing in all the following examples.

(*e*) (Two Credits.) — Parse *make* and *grow.*

(*f*) (Two Credits.) — Parse *earth* and *comes.*

(*g*) (Two Credits.) — Parse *yet* and *thee.*

(*h*) (Two Credits.) — The first six lines form what kind of an element or modifier? What does it modify?

(*i*) (Two Credits.) — What is "When thoughts of the last bitter hour?" etc.

(*j*) (Two Credits.) — What is "Yet, a few days, and thee the all-beholding sun?" etc. S.

SET III.

TOTAL: TWELVE QUESTIONS — ONE HUNDRED CREDITS.

Eight Questions — Five Credits Each.

1. Write a sentence of four words only, containing an adjective, a noun, a verb, and an adverb.

2. Analyze the sentence written, and parse each word.

3. Name three ways of forming the plurals of nouns, and give an example of each.

4. Give a synopsis of the verb *go* in the indicative mode, third person, singular number, interrogative form.

5. Write a compound sentence.

6. Write a sentence containing a verb in the passive voice.

7. Principal parts of the following verbs: *break, burst, work, drink?*

8. Correct the following sentences: (No credits unless the *reasons* for correcting are given). "There was no men killed." "They said it was her."

Twelve Credits.

9. "The evil that men do lives after them."

(*a*) What kind of a sentence is the preceding?

(*b*) Of what is *evil* the subject?

(*c*) What part of speech is *that* and in what case is it?

(*d*) Is *do* a transitive, or an intransitive verb?

Twelve Credits.

10. "So let it be with Cæsar."

(*a*) What kind of a sentence?

(*b*) Parse *let.*

(*c*) Parse *it.*

(*d*) Parse *be.*

Sixteen Credits—One Credit off for Each Error Uncorrected.

11. Correct the capitals, spelling, punctuation, and violations of grammatical rules of the following sentence:—

"the productions of the american soil and climate has poured out their abundance of luxurys for the tables of the rich and of nescesarys for the sustainance of the poor birds and animals of beauty and value has been added to the european stocks and transplantations from the unequalled riches of our forests has mingled itself with the elms and ashes and druidical oaks of england."—WEBSTER.

Twenty Credits.

12. "So live, that when thy summons comes to join
The innumerable caravan which moves
To that mysterious realm where each shall take
His chamber in the silent halls of death,
Thou go not, like the quarry slave at night

Scourged to his dungeon, but, sustained and soothed
By an unfaltering trust, approach thy grave
Like one who wraps the drapery of his couch
About him and lies down to pleasant dreams."

Thanatopsis.

2. (*a*) What kind of a sentence is the preceding stanza, and why?

(*b*) What kind of poetry is it called, and why?

(*c*) In what mood is *live*, and what is its subject?

(*d*) Parse *go*.

(*e*) Conjugate *go* in the mood and tense in which it is found here.

(*f*) Parse *approach*.

(*g*) Parse *sustained*.

(*h*) Parse *one*.

(*i*) What kind of a clause is "Who wraps," etc.?

(*j*) What kind of a clause is "When thy summons," etc., and what does it modify? S.

SET IV.

TEN QUESTIONS — TEN CREDITS EACH.

1. Write a complex sentence, and analyze it.

2. Name the five elements of a sentence. Give an example of a sentence containing all the elements.

3 and 4. Analyze the following sentence: —

"When, in the course of human events, it becomes necessary for one people to dissolve the political bands which have connected them with another, and to assume among the powers of the earth the separate and equal station to which the laws of nature and of nature's God entitle them, a decent respect to the opinions of mankind requires that they should declare the causes which impel them to the separation."

5. Write all the transitive verbs in the preceding sentence, with their subjects and objects.

6. Parse *that,* in the last clause of the sentence above. Parse *entitle,* and *to assume.*

7. Compare *worse, little, first.* Decline *us, which.* Give the principal parts of *get, ought,* and *drink.*

8. Write a sentence to illustrate each of the different moods.

9. Give a rule for the use of each of the following points, and an example to illustrate: Comma, semicolon, caret, quotation marks.

10. Write a compound sentence composed of two complex clauses. S.

SET V.

TWENTY QUESTIONS—FIVE CREDITS EACH.

1. Write a synopsis of the verb *to lay* in the indicative and potential modes, third person, singular number, active and passive voices. Synopsis of the same in the indicative mode, first person, singular number, interrogative-negative form.

2. Principal parts of the following verbs: *to fly, to flee, to cleave,* (*to split*), *to dare,* (*to venture*), *to chide, to work.*

3. State in what cases the letter *s* is omitted in forming the possessive case, and give examples.

4. What is the difference between a verb and a noun?

5. When is the relative *that* used in preference to *who* or *which?*

6. Give an example in which *as* is used as a relative pronoun.

7. Correct the following, and give the reasons for correcting:—

Nothing is more preferable than a good character.

Daniel Webster, and Lewis Cass, also, were born in New Hampshire.

I expect the books were sent yesterday.
I differ from him in opinion.

8. "Than who none higher sat:" parse *who.*

9. Give at least three rules for the use of the period in punctuation, and an example to illustrate each.

10. "He was made too much of by his mother:" parse *was made too much of.*

11. Write the plurals of the following, giving both forms when there are two: *lasso, wharf, two, Henry, index, pea, die, gallows, fish, gymnasium, Mr., handful, erratum, folio, who, scarf, emphasis, focus.*

12. Decline, in the singular and plural, the following: *man, lady, which, John, I, it, that.*

13. What is the difference between a preposition and conjunction?

14. Punctuate and capitalize the following:—

> "what sort of eyes can you have got said he
> why very good ones friend as you may see
> yes I perceive the clearness of the ball
> pray let me ask you can you read at all."

15. Write a compound sentence, and analyze it according to any system of analysis you have learned.

16. Give three examples of idiomatic constructions in the English language.

17. "Talent is something, but tact is everything." Analyze the sentence, and parse *something.*

18. Give an example to illustrate each of the six tenses.

19. Which is the better usage in proper names ending with *s*, using an additional *s* or the apostrophe only? Would you write *Willis' Poems*, or *Willis's Poems?* In what cases does the letter *s* add another syllable in pronunciation?

20. What direction can you give for the use of *shall* and *will* to express future time? S.

SET VI.

TEN QUESTIONS — TEN CREDITS EACH.

1. Give a synopsis of the verb *write*, in the indicative mode, passive voice, declarative form, third person, singular number; and a synopsis of the verb *run*, in the indicative and potential modes, interrogative form, first person, singular number.

2. Give the principal parts of the following verbs: *dive, strive, weave, build, lie, lay, hew, burst, set, sit, swim, eat, drink.*

3. Write the possessive plural of *child, woman, it, who, thou, ox.*

4. Write a sentence containing the word *that*, used as a relative, as an adjective, and as a conjunction; and state when the relative *that* is used in preference to *who* or *which.*

5. Parse each word in the following sentence: "Teach me what is right."

6. Analyze the following sentence: "Education is the only interest worthy the deep controlling anxiety of a truly thoughtful man."

7. Mention the principal rules for the use of the comma in punctuation.

8. Correct the following: —

"Your brother came right straight into the room and said to my sister and I whom were sitting there I am tired and must lay down to rest me and when he was laying down we tryed to lie a veil over his face to cover it up out of sight."

9. What is an elementary sound? A letter? A phrase? A clause? A simple sentence?

10. Construct sentences in which a word, a phrase, and a clause, shall be used as the subject of a verb. S.

SET VII.

ONE HUNDRED CREDITS.

1. What is the difference between analysis and parsing?

2. Decline *thou, who, which, that, I, it.*

3. Write the present tense, past tense, and past participle of the following verbs, giving both forms, when two are used: *ride, catch, load, eat, ring, burst, dive, get, thrust, greet, aim, sit, work, dig, dream.* (Write the principal parts in three perpendicular columns.)

4. Compare *chief, much, old, former, far, forth, ill, next, lest, hinder, up, lovely.*

5. Give three important rules in orthography, and words to illustrate each.

6. Write the possessive plural of *woman, loaf, it, thou,* and *ox;* the plural of *handful, money,* the letter *t, focus, monsieur, chrysalis, genus, miasma.*

7. Write two rules about the formation of the possessive case with the use of the apostrophe *s*, and illustrate by examples.

8. Analyze the following sentence, and parse each word: "Teach me what is true."

9. How many words in the English language? How many in common use?

10. Give two rules for the use of the comma in punctuation, and examples to illustrate; one rule for the use of the semicolon, with an example to illustrate.

11. Define collective and verbal nouns, and write a sentence containing an example of each.

12. Write five prefixes of Saxon origin, five of Latin, and five of Greek, giving the meaning of each.

13. State which of the following expressions are

allowable according to good usage, which are not, and correct the faulty ones :—

(*a*) I had as lief go as not.
(*b*) Serious consequences had liked to have resulted.
(*c*) I had rather not do it.
(*d*) You had better write.
(*e*) We differ with him about that sentence.
(*f*) It ought to be put a stop to.
(*g*) The ship was soon lost sight of.

14. Give five directions to a pupil to be observed in writing a composition.

15. Correct the following sentences :—

The cavalry were more feared than the infantry. Neither poverty nor riches were injurious. This people have spoken. The Board of Education has granted a certificate. The Board of Trustees has agreed to settle the difficulty among themselves. S.

SET VIII.

TEN QUESTIONS—TEN CREDITS EACH.

1. Write a compound sentence containing an objective clause.

2. Of what person must *nouns*, used as subject or object of verbs, *always* be?

3. Compare *late* and *old*.
Give positives of *worse*.
Give positives of *most*.
Give superlatives of *fore*.
Give superlatives of *far*.
Give superlatives of *up*.

4. Correct the following sentences (no credits unless the reasons are given) :—

Let no one deceive themselves. Iron is more useful

than all the metals. Every one of these theories are exploded. It was Joseph, him whom Pharaoh promoted.

5. Parse the italicised words in the following:—

"That he should refuse is not *strange*."
[What is the subject of "is?"]
"To die a *hero* is sublime."

6. Give the principal parts of *sit* and *set; rise* and *raise;* and make sentences containing each of them used properly in the past perfect tense.

7. How is the conjugation of English verbs effected? Illustrate each method.

8. "Much depends upon who the commissioners are;" parse *upon*. "I know him to be your friend;" parse *him*. "The cake is too rich for the child to eat;" parse *to eat*.

9. Give the past tense, indicative mode of the verb *do*. Potential mode, past perfect tense of *go*. Indicative mode, present perfect tense of *lie* (to recline.)

"But this very day,
An honest man, my neighbor,—there he stands,—
Was struck—struck like a dog, by one who wore
The badge of Ursine; because, forsooth,
He tossed not high his ready cap in air,
Nor lifted up his voice in servile shouts,
At sight of that great ruffian! Be we men,
And suffer such dishonor?"

(*a*) Parse *But*.
(*b*) In what case is *day?*
(*c*) What is the subject of *was struck?*
(*d*) Analyze *there he stands*.
(*e*) Parse *forsooth*.
(*f*) Parse *high*.
(*g*) Parse *dog*.

(*h*) Analyze "Be we men, and suffer such dishonor?"

(*i*) Parse *Be*.

(*j*) In what case is *men?*

SET IX.

1. Define simple, complex, and compound elements, giving an example of each.

2. Give the various uses of the word *that*, with illustrations.

3. Write five rules for the use of capital letters.

4. When is *to* of the infinitive mode.

5. Give a complete classification of sentences, and define each class.

6. Define analysis and parsing, as used in grammar.

7. Analyze the sentence, "My mother died when I was very young."

8. Write a short letter.

9. In the sentence, "That life is long which answers life's great end;" parse *that*, *is*, *long*, *which end*.

10. Write the possessive plural of *other*, *she*, *children;* possessive singular of *conscience;* express, by the use of the possessive, the joint ownership of a boat by John and James.

SET X.

TEN QUESTIONS — TEN CREDITS EACH.

1. What is the difference between simple, complex, and compound sentences? Give an example of each kind.

2. Name four cases in which the pronoun *that* is used in preference to *who* or *which*.

3. What distinctions can you mention in the use of *shall* and *will?*

4. What are the principal elements of an English sentence, and what is their natural order?

5. What kind of a sentence is the following: "Let me see what you have"? Parse *what* and *see.*

6. "Sink or swim, live or die, survive or perish, I am for the Declaration." What kind of sentence, and why? Parse *sink.*

7. Write a synopsis of the verb *drink,* in the indicative and potential modes.

8. Write a sentence to illustrate each of the modes and each of the forms of the verb.

9. Correct the following:—

"We will be delighted when the examination shall have been finished. Either I or he are to blame."

10. Write three general rules for the use of the comma, two for the semicolon, and two for the period, and give a sentence to illustrate. S.

SET XI.

TEN QUESTIONS — TEN CREDITS EACH.

1. Give all the principal parts of the verbs of which the following are parts: *was, gone, fought, decide, talked.*

2. Parse all the *irregular verbs* in the following sentence:—

"The men fought well, but they were unable to endure the fatigue of long marches."

3. Parse all the *relative pronouns* in the following sentence:—

"That man who fails while attempting to do right, is more to be respected than he who succeeds in doing what is wrong."

4. Correct the following sentences, if they need correction, and give reasons for correcting:—

(*a*) Between you and I, this must be kept secret.

(*b*) You and not I, am to blame.

(*c*) The larger part of the coins was destroyed.

5. Name and define the properties of pronouns.

6. Analyze the following sentence:—

"The dipping paddle echoes far
And flashes in the moonlight gleam."

7. Define — subject-nominative, predicate-verb, simple subject, compound predicate.

8. Conjugate the verb *sleep* through the present and the past tenses of the indicative mode.

9. Define the difference between a transitive and an intransitive verb.

10. Give a sentence that shall contain an adjective irregularly compared; also a sentence containing an adverb which is compared.

SET XII.

TEN QUESTIONS—TEN CREDITS EACH.

1. Explain the following terms as used in grammar, illustrating each by an example: *voice, tense, person, case, predicate.*

2. Why is a personal pronoun so called?

3. Give examples of the correct use of the verbs, *lie, lay, sit,* and *set,* in the present, past, and present perfect tenses, indicative mode.

4. Write the plural of *loaf, wife, dwarf, cherub, lily, monkey, turkey, handful, grotto, staff, stave.*

Give the general rules for forming the plural of nouns. Also exceptions which apply to any of the preceding words.

5. Compare the following adjectives: *better, worse holy, next, first, last, less, ill, supreme, blue.*

6. Correct the following sentences:—

I have less books than you. He was more active but not so studious as John. You should have let that remained where it was. Who had I ought to have given this to? If any one asks about me, tell them I am nicely. Have either of you seen him? I am sorry not to have seen you. He should never marry a woman in high life that has no money.

7. Parse the *italicized* words in the following passage: —

> "A prompt decisive *man*, *no* breath
> Our father wasted; '*Boys*, a *path*!'
> *Well pleased* (for *when* did *farmer* boy,
> *Count such* a summons less than joy?)
> Our *buskins on* our feet we draw." WHITTIER.

8. Analyze the first sentence in the above passage.

9. Paraphrase the following passage, expanding it in thought and expression as much as you please: —

> "Life's more than breath, and the quick round of blood —
> We live in deeds not years; in thoughts, not breaths —
> We should count time by heart-throbs. He most lives
> Who thinks most — feels the noblest — acts the best.
> Life's but a means unto an end."

10. How many sentences in the preceding stanza, and what kind of sentences are they?

SET XIII.

TEN QUESTIONS — TEN CREDITS EACH.

1. Write the plural of *money*, *lady*, *berry*, *wharf*, *elf*, *gulf*, *thief*, *cameo*, *focus*, *stratum*, *vortex*.

Write the relative pronouns, and state how they differ from personal pronouns.

3. State how adjectives are compared, and compare *ill*, *many*, *near*, *late*, *old*.

4. Write the principal parts of *bring*, *buy*, *chide*, *clothe*, *drink*, *fly*, *lay*, *seethe*, *throw*.

5. Parse the words in italics in the following sentences: —

Forth in the pleasing Spring, Thy *beauty* walks, Thy

tenderness and love. *Wide*, flush the *fields*. The softening air is *balm*. *Echo*, the *mountain* round. The forest *smiles*, and every sense and every heart is joy.

6. The house is my *own*; and I *own* my *horse*.

7. He was displeased, on *account* of *my being* a *friend* to his enemy.

8. "For *who*, to dumb forgetfulness, a *prey*,
This pleasing anxious *being* e'er *resigned*,
Left the warm precincts of the cheerful day,
Nor *cast* one longing, *lingering* look behind.

9. Analyze the following sentence, and parse the words in italics: "She hath *done what* she *could*."

10. Correct the following sentences:—

Which is the larger city, New York or Paris? John is not as tall as James. The teacher learned his class French. What time did he say it was? I shall come to Providence this week.

SET XIV.

FIVE QUESTIONS—TWENTY CREDITS EACH.

1. Punctuate the following sentences:—

(*a*) He being dead yet speaketh

(*b*) Morning is the best time to study my beloved children

(*c*) The sun having risen we parted on our journey

(*d*) I rise Mr President to a point of order

(*e*) Some writers divide the history of the world into four ages the golden age the silver age the bronze age and the iron age

(*f*) Of all our senses the sight is the most perfect

(*g*) Stones grow vegetables grow and live animals grow live and feed

2. Punctuate the following sentences, and make the necessary corrections in regard to capitals:—

(*a*) the scots at break of day entered the castle

(*b*) the man when he saw this departed

(*c*) he saith unto him feed my sheep

3. Make the necessary corrections in the following sentences: —

(*a*) Every one of the witnesses testify to the same thing.

(*b*) Either James or William have to stay at home. George learned him music.

(*c*) He laid down to take a nap.

(*d*) He was much effected by the news.

(*e*) He labored hard but affected nothing.

(*f*) Four month's interest are due on the bonds.

(*g*) Neither thou nor I art to blame.

4. Parse the words in italics in the following extract: —

> "Now *came still* evening on, and twilight gray
> Had in her sober livery all *things* clad;
> *Silence* accompanied; for *beast* and bird,
> They to their grassy couch, these to their nests
> Were slunk; *all* but the wakeful *nightingale*,
> She all *night* long her amorous *descant* sung."

5. Analyze the following sentences, and parse the words in italics: —

(*a*) There is no doubt of his *being* a great *scholar*.

(*b*) It is a *disgrace to be* the *author* of such a report.

SET XV.

TEN QUESTIONS — VALUE FIVE EACH.

1. Punctuate the following sentences; correct all the errors in them; and write them out grammatically, if they are ungrammatical: —

1. i should not have Went if he had not have expected me.

2. beleive me i did not think to have receive such News.

3. The derevation of these Words is unsertain.

2. Write the principal parts of the following verbs: *quit, rid, get, thrive, weave, sit, stride, hew, set, burst.*

3. Write a sentence with the verb *to undo* in the passive voice, potential mode, past perfect tense, in the third person, plural.

4. Write the possessive singular and the possessive plural of the following nouns: *man, child, body, valley.*

5. Write the plural of *shelf, dwarf, coachful, chimney, son-in-law, genus, salmon, dozen, idea, gold,* the letter *t*, and the figure 6.

6. How are the passive voice and the progressive form of a verb composed?

7. Write a sentence with the verb *to sleep* in the infinitive mode, present perfect tense, passive voice.

8. Why is "You had not ought" ungrammatical?

9. Of what does syntax treat?

10. What do you mean by an *idiom?* Give an example.

S.

GEOGRAPHY.

SET I.

TWENTY QUESTIONS — FIVE CREDITS EACH.

1. WHAT is supposed to be the reason why the earth is flattened at the poles?

2. Name the two great mountain systems of the United States; the four great rivers; the largest four cities; and the three great sea-ports.

3. Name the two great mountain ranges, the four great cities, and the four great rivers of Asia.

4. Why does so little rain fall on that part of South America west of the Andes mountain range?

5. What is the length of the longest night at the line of the Equator? on the line of the Arctic Circle? at the North Pole?

6. Why is the climate cold in the Polar regions and hot in the Equatorial regions?

7. Name a large city noted for the manufacture of cotton cloth; one noted for its silks; one noted for its iron works.

8. Name three animals peculiar to the Torrid Zone; three peculiar to the Temperate Zone; three peculiar to the Frigid Zone.

9. How do the products of the northern part of the United States differ from those of the southern?

10. What part of the United States is a plateau or highland? Why does it have less rain than the valley of the Mississippi?

11. Name the two great rivers of South America; two of Africa; four of Europe.

12. What country produces the most cotton? the most sugar? the most rice? the most coffee?

13. What country is the greatest manufacturing country in the world? What country manufactures the most silk?

14. What country exports the greatest quantity of hides? wines? wool? tea?

15. Four leading exports of California?

16. What is the use of latitude and longitude?

17. What commercial advantages has New York City? Boston? San Francisco?

18. State by what great commercial routes you can now travel round the world, starting from San Francisco.

19. What articles are exchanged between the mining States and the agricultural States of the Mississippi valley? between the manufacturing States and the mining States?

20. What country in the world has the longest and most numerous lines of railroad. S.

SET II.

TEN QUESTIONS — TEN CREDITS EACH.

1. What large cities are situated on the Mississippi and its tributaries?

2. Define latitude, longitude, and meridians.

3. What is the Gulf Stream? where does it flow? and what effect does it have on the climate of certain countries?

4. Give the population, in round numbers, of the most powerful State in the Union, and mention five of its principal cities.

5. Name the three great rivers of North America which flow into the Pacific.

6. In what respects does California differ from Massachusetts?

7. Name four cities noted for their great elevation above the level of the sea.

8. State the situation of the following places: Marseilles, Yokohama, Quito, Hong Kong, Mt. Etna, Mt. Hecla, Mt. Everest, Lake Tchad, Yukon River, Hobart Town.

9. Why does so little rain fall in Peru, and so much in the basin of the Amazon? Why so little in the Sahara?

10. Give some illustrations of the effect of climate on the human race and on vegetation. S.

SET III.

TWENTY QUESTIONS — FIVE CREDITS EACH.

1. Bound Europe. Give its area, and five most important cities.

2. What are the area and population of the United States?

3. What are the latitude and longitude of Washington City?

4. Describe the river Danube; the Amoor; the Niger; Orinoco.

5. Why is the climate of the California coast milder than that of the corresponding latitude on the Atlantic coast?

6. Name the largest rivers, three principal capes, three largest cities of Great Britain.

7. What imaginary lines would be removed from the surface of the globe if its axis were perpendicular to the plane of its orbit, and what would be the effect upon the seasons, and on the length of days and nights?

8. If the rotary motion of the earth were to cease,

what change would be made in the distribution of water on the surface of the globe? What change if the equatorial diameter were made equal to the polar?

9. Mention some of the causes which produce oceanic currents, and name any of the effects of such currents.

10. Bound China. Give its population, and its two principal rivers, sea-ports, and cities.

11. What are the principal points of difference and of resemblance between the English Parliament and the Congress of the United States?

12. State the situation of Bordeaux, Havre, Marseilles, and Cherbourg.

13. What are the principal points of difference and resemblance, in respect to physical features, between Africa and South America?

14. Locate the following places: Vicksburg, Atlanta, Nassau, Manila, and Bombay.

15. What are glaciers, and in what countries are they found?

16. In which hemisphere is Iceland — eastern or western? In which are New Zealand and Australia?

17. How does Australia compare in size with Europe, and what are some of the animals peculiar to it?

18. Name the three principal cities, and two largest rivers of Italy.

19. What large cities in the Torrid Zone, and what islands are crossed by the Equator?

20. What are the great natural divisions of the United States? S.

SET IV.

TEN QUESTIONS — FIVE CREDITS EACH.

1. What is the cause of day and night, and of the change of seasons?

2. Which has at any time the longer day, Quito or St. Petersburg?

3. Which of the grand divisions of the earth is the largest? which the most populous? which most fertile? which has the highest mountains? which the largest rivers? which, the most inland seas?

4. What is the latitude of the Arctic circle? of the Tropic of Cancer? of Cape Horn? of Panama? of San Francisco? of New York?

5. What are the principal rivers which flow into the Atlantic Ocean? Pacific? Arctic? Antarctic?

6. What meridian divides the Eastern from the Western Hemisphere?

7. Bound Australia.

8. Where is Honolulu? Manila? Canton? Sydney? Acapulco?

9. Where is Chicago? Cincinnati? St. Louis? Sacramento? Sitka?

FIVE QUESTIONS — TEN CREDITS EACH.

10. Draw a contrast between productions and climate of California and Massachusetts.

11. Where is Pike's Peak? Harper's Ferry? San Juan Island? Yukon River?

12. What railway lines would you pass over in travelling by railroad from Boston to San Francisco?

13. What is the principal sea-port city of France? England? Austria? Russia? China? Brazil? Japan?

14. When are the days and nights of equal length all over the globe?

15. Which is the highest mountain peak on the globe? the largest island? the largest city? the largest empire? the most powerful nation? the ruling race of men? S.

SET V.

TEN QUESTIONS — TEN CREDITS EACH.

1. Define latitude and longitude. State the length of a degree, and show how a degree of latitude compares with a degree of longitude.

2. Give the width of each zone in degrees.

3. State the departments into which the government of the United States is divided.

4. Mention the State that excels in each of the following particulars: (1) population; (2) number of good harbors; (3) production of salt; (4) of cotton; (5) of wheat; (6) of iron; (7) of copper; (8) of wine; (9) of sugar; (10) in variety of manufactures.

5. Name five important commercial articles which are imported from South America.

6. Name and locate five important cities of Europe, — no two to be in the same country.

7. What comparison can you draw between Japan and Great Britain?

8. If you should go by water from Chicago to Constantinople, what waters would be passed over?

9. Name and locate five mountain ranges in Europe, and five seas in or around Asia.

10. Where and what are the following? (1) Andorra; (2) Mecca; (3) Madagascar; (4) Honolulu; (5) Victoria; (6) Potosi; (7) Wyoming; (8) Key West.

SET VI.

TEN QUESTIONS — TEN CREDITS EACH.

1. What are the products of the frigid zone?

2. Give the population of the State of New York, and mention five of its principal cities.

3. Bound Mexico, name its principal seaports, and give the situation of the cities of Mexico and Vera Cruz.

4. What is the population, in round numbers, of New York City? of London? of Paris?

5. What is the estimated population of the globe? of China? What is the relative proportion of the Caucasian and Mongolian races?

6. What are the principal rivers which flow into the Pacific Ocean?

7. What are the principal possessions of Great Britain in various parts of the world?

8. Bound Asia, and name its five principal rivers and cities.

9. What are the principal seas in and around Europe.

10. Bound France, and give the situation of Paris, Bordeaux, Havre, and Marseilles. S.

SET VII.

TOTAL: FIFTEEN QUESTIONS — ONE HUNDRED CREDITS.

Ten Questions — Five Credits Each.

1. Define ecliptic and solstice.

2. Define latitude and longitude.

3. Locate Strasbourg; Damascus; Waterloo.

4. Where are Mt. Ararat? Mt. St. Elias? Stromboli?

5. Name the Territories of the United States.

6. Mention three countries in which is raised most of the flax used in the manufacture of linen.

7. Name the three largest cities of the United States; of Europe; of Asia.

8. Where is the coffee tree most extensively cultivated? sugar cane? the pepper plant? cinnamon? the cotton plant?

9. What section of the United States has the greatest amount of rain? the least? What contrast is presented by the climate of the Atlantic and Pacific coasts?

10. What part of North America is a lowland? Which grand division has the greatest mass of table-land.

Five Questions — Ten Credits Each.

1. Describe the Gulf Stream, and tell what effect it has on the climate of Europe.

2. What is the cause of the change of seasons, and of the length of day and night?

3. Name four animals peculiar to the Temperate Zone; four to the Torrid; three to the Frigid. What causes wind? In what direction do trade-winds blow?

4. Why does the quantity of rain decrease as we recede from the Equator? Why less in the interior than on the coast? Why more in mountainous than in level districts?

5. When it is noon in San Francisco, what time is it at a place 70° east of it? 75° west of it?

SET VIII.

FIVE QUESTIONS — THREE CREDITS EACH.

1. What is the highest mountain in the United States? Name and give the approximate height of the highest mountain on the globe.

2. Name the two greatest river basins in the world.

3. What countries are crossed by the Equator?

4. To what race do the Arabs belong? The Hindoos? The Esquimaux?

5. Where is Manila? Mention two states of Mexico.

Five Questions — Five Credits Each.

6. Name and describe the longest river, and locate the largest city, in each of the grand divisions.

7. Name the provinces of which the Chinese Empire is composed.

8. Name the ten principal commercial cities of the world.

9. Describe the formation of the coral islands.

10. To what zone is the growth of such islands chiefly confined? Mention two islands of volcanic origin.

Six Questions — Ten Credits Each.

11. By what are tides caused? What is the greatest height to which tides rise?

12. How is a tidal wave created?

13. Mention four causes which affect the temperature of a place.

14. On which side of the continents do the isotherms run farthest north? Why?

15. Which has the more rain, Africa or South America? Why?

16. Explain the origin, direction, and limits of the trade-winds.

SET IX.

FIFTEEN QUESTIONS — FIVE CREDITS EACH.

1. Why are the Tropics and Polar circles $23\frac{1}{2}°$ from the Equator and the Poles?

2. What is the length of the longest day at the Polar circles and at the Equator?

3. Name the grand divisions of the earth, in the order of their population.

4. Name the highest mountain peak and the largest river, in each of the grand divisions.

5. Name the principal plateaux of Asia and North America, and the principal plains of South America, Europe, and Africa.

6. What are the circumstances which affect the climate of a place?

7. Describe the Gulf Stream, and its modifying effect on the climate of any part of the globe.

8. Name the races of men, and the principal countries in which each race is found.

9. Define ecliptic and meridian.

10. Name in order of size the largest ten cities of the globe.

11. What is the latitude of London? New York? Quito?

12. Name the principal mountain ranges of the United States, and five of the principal rivers.

13. Name the largest four river basins of the globe.

14. Name a river and town in each of the following Territories: Kansas, Washington, New Mexico, and Dakota.

15. Name the largest four eastern, and the largest four western branches of the Mississippi.

SET X.

TEN QUESTIONS—TEN CREDITS EACH.

1. State the width in degrees of the Torrid, Temperate, and Frigid Zones.

2. Why do no large streams in South America flow into the Pacific Ocean?

3. Which is further north, Cincinnati or Rome? Newfoundland or England?

4. State the prevailing direction of the principal mountain chains in each of the continents.

5. What are Spitzbergen, St. Helena, New Zealand, Vancouver, and Mauritius?

6. Name the "Five Great Powers" of Europe, and the form of government in each.

7. In which zones are the most highly civilized nations found, and why?

8. From what countries do we obtain the following articles: (1) cloves; (2) nutmegs; (3) gutta-percha; (4) platina; (5) tin.

9. Does Mercator's Map show the true relative sizes of those countries near the Equator, and those remote from it, and why?

10. Name ten seas bordering Asia.

SET XI.

FIFTEEN QUESTIONS — FIVE CREDITS EACH.

1. What circles on the globe would be omitted if the axis of the earth were perpendicular to the plane of its orbit?

2. What angle does the axis of the earth make with the plane of its orbit?

3. What is meant by the meridian of a place?

4. What is the zodiac? The ecliptic?

5. Why are the Polar circles and the Tropics drawn where they are upon the globe?

6. Through what waters would you sail in going from Pittsburg, Pennsylvania, to Pekin?

7. Define an isothermal line. What is the line of perpetual snow.

8. What is the cause of the trade-winds?

9. Name the different classes of winds, and give an example under each.

10. Why is it warmer on the Pacific than on the Atlantic coast of the United States, in the same latitude?

11. How are the wet and dry seasons of California produced?

12. Describe the principal currents of the ocean and explain their causes.

13. What are the area, boundaries, and population of the United States?

14. In what parts of the world are the Mongolian race found?

15. What are their characteristics, physical and mental?

HISTORY OF THE UNITED STATES.

SET I.

TWENTY QUESTIONS — FIVE CREDITS EACH.

1. WHAT was the government of the American Colonies prior to 1775, how were their rights guaranteed, to what extent did they have the power of self-government, and to what extent were they controlled by the king of England?

2. What discoveries and settlements did the French make in North America, and what wars arose in consequence?

3. What were the "Articles of Confederation," when were they adopted, and why? What were their radical defects?

4. When and where did the first Colonial Congress assemble, why was it called, and what was done?

5. What action did the first Continental Congress take? What distinguished men were members of it?

6. What were the more immediate causes of the American Revolution? The more remote?

7. In what way did France aid the Colonies in establishing their independence, and how was that aid secured?

8. What were the names of the first two great political parties formed in the United States after the adoption of the Constitution, and what were the distinctive principles of each?

9. What was the occasion of the "Nullification Act" in South Carolina, in Jackson's administration, and what concessions were made by the government to keep that State in the Union?

10. What was the alleged reason for the secession of the Southern States?

11. What States seceded, and how and when did they organize a government?

12. When and how was the War of Secession begun? When and how was it ended?

13. Name five great battles of the war, and the year in which each was fought.

14. When was the "Emancipation Proclamation" issued, on what grounds, what did it provide, and what was its effect on the nation?

15. Name the principal victories won by General Grant; by Sherman; by Sheridan; by Lee.

16. How did Congress provide means to raise money to carry on the war?

17. What is the estimated loss of men, including the killed in battle, those who died in hospitals and prisons, on both sides, during this war?

18. Give a brief account of the Battle of Bull Run.

19. Give the names of five distinguished Union officers killed in battle.

20. What is the national debt incurred during the war?

S.

SET II.

TWENTY QUESTIONS—FIVE CREDITS EACH.

1. How did the restoration of King Charles II. influence the settlement of the American Colonies?

2. What important event took place in England in 1688? What caused it, and how was the news received in America?

3. What were the distinguishing traits and political opinions of the English Puritans in the time of Cromwell?

4. What discoveries and what settlements did the French make in North America, and what wars arose in consequence?

5. What were the Articles of Confederation, when were they adopted, and why? What were their radical defects?

6. When and where did the first Continental Congress assemble? Why was it called, and what was done?

7. Name three distinguished men who were members of the First Continental Congress.

8. Specify the principal grievances of the Colonies against the mother country.

9. What were the navigation laws?

10. What men took a prominent part in the preliminary movements of the American Revolution?

11. Who was king of England in 1776, and what was his character? Who was his prime minister?

12. What British statesman opposed the American war?

13. What part did Robert Morris, Benjamin Franklin, and Thomas Jefferson take in the War of the Revolution?

14. Give some account of the plot to supersede Washington as commander-in-chief of the army.

15. How did Congress provide means to carry on the war?

16. What was eventually done with the depreciated currency?

17. What were the names of the first two political parties formed in the United States after the adoption of the Constitution, and what were the distinctive principles of each?

18. When was the Battle of Gettysburg fought? What number of troops was engaged? What was the loss in killed and wounded?

19. Give a short account of the Battle of Chattanooga, and the storming of Lookout Mountain.

20. How was New Orleans captured? S.

SET III.

TOTAL: FIFTEEN QUESTIONS—ONE HUNDRED CREDITS.

Ten Questions—Five Credits Each.

1. When and where was California first settled by a civilized race?

2. Mention two leading events of each of the following administrations: Lincoln's; Buchanan's; Jackson's; Washington's.

3. When and where were the first and last battles of the war of the rebellion fought?

4. When and where was the Battle of Gettysburg fought, who were the commanders of the respective armies, and what was the result?

5. What was the *Alabama*, and what is meant by the "Alabama claims?"

6. What amendments have been made to the Constitution, since the close of the late civil war?

7. Name the two principal battles of the War of 1812, or the second war with England, and state the result.

8. Name four important battles of the war with Mexico, and state what territory was acquired by the United States as the result of that war.

9. Who was the most distinguished American naval commander, during the War of the Revolution? of 1812? of the Rebellion?

10. What part did the following distinguished men

take in the American Revolution: Thomas Jefferson; John Adams; Robert Morris; Alexander Hamilton?

Five Questions — Ten Credits Each.

11. For what is each of the following places distinguished in American History: St. Augustine; Annapolis; Charleston; New Orleans; Guilford Court House; Monmouth?

12. When and by whom was each of the following States settled: Virginia; Rhode Island; New York; Maryland?

13. By whom was Louisiana settled, and how did it become a part of the United States? Florida?

14. Name four orators distinguished in American history; four statesmen; four generals; two historians; two poets.

15. Draw a contrast between the United States at the close of the War of the Revolution and at the present time. S.

SET IV.

TEN QUESTIONS — FIVE CREDITS EACH.

1. Where and when was the first permanent settlement made within the present limits of the United States?

2. Name two of the early French settlements in America; two of the Spanish; two of the English.

3. When, where, and by whom was Utah first settled?

4. Mention one important event connected with the settlement of Virginia; of Massachusetts; of Maryland; of New York; of Georgia.

5. Name four colonial wars, and mention one leading event in each.

6. Where did the first Continental Congress meet? Mention two of its enactments.

7. Name four important battles in which the Americans were successful, during the Revolution.

8. Name four battles in which Washington commanded in person.

9. What caused the War of 1812, and during whose presidential administration did it occur?

10. How long did the war of secession last? When and where did Lee's army surrender? S.

SET V.

TEN QUESTIONS — TEN CREDITS EACH.

1. How are United States Senators elected, and for what time? How are members of the House of Representatives elected, and what is the basis of representation?

2. When was the Constitution of the United States adopted? what cause led to its adoption? who framed it? and who presided over the convention?

3. What was the Compromise of 1850?

4. What causes led to the secession of the Southern States and who were the leading men in that movement?

5. What was the most important battle of the War of 1812? when and where was it fought, and what were the results gained by it?

6. Give some account of the naval battles of the frigate *Constitution* and of the iron-clad *Monitor*.

7. What connection had Robert Morris, Thomas Jefferson, and Benjamin Franklin, with American history?

8. Who was Daniel Webster? Henry Clay? John C. Calhoun? James Buchanan?

9. Name the principal battles of the War of Secession.

10. What discoveries were made by the Cabots? S.

SET VI.

1. By whom was the Mississippi discovered? Where? When?

2. Give the date and place of the earliest settlements in the United States?

(*a*) By the English.

(*b*) By the Spanish.

(*c*) By the Dutch.

3. What was the chief cause of the war in America between the French and English?

What part did the Indians take?

Name the military leaders on both sides.

4. What provisions were made for education in the early history of Massachusetts?

5. What was the "Bill of Rights?" By whom passed? Give its date.

6. How long did the Revolution continue? Name the first and last battles.

7. State the important differences between the Articles of Confederation and the Constitution of the United States.

8. What officers constitute the Cabinet of the President?

9. When are parties entitled to trial by jury?

10. What rights has the accused in respect to witnesses?

SET VII.

TWENTY QUESTIONS — FIVE CREDITS EACH.

1. What induced Columbus to attempt the discovery of a western continent?

2. Who discovered Mexico? Who conquered it? About what time?

3. Mention three discoveries made by the English: by the French.

4. What difficulties did the early Colonial settlers encounter?

5. About what time does the Colonial history of the United States commence? When does it end?

6. Why did many of the Indian tribes unite with the French in opposing the Colonies? Mention the place of the battle which put an end to the French power in North America.

7. When and where did the first Continental Congress meet? What did this Congress do?

8. Why was the battle of Saratoga a decisive one?

9. What was the condition of the country from the time when peace was proclaimed to the inauguration of Washington?

10. Who was President during the War of 1812? What battle terminated the war?

11. What was the Missouri Compromise?

12. Name two events of Jackson's administration.

13. During whose administration did the Mexican War occur? What were the causes which led to the Mexican War?

15. Mention five important battles of the Mexican War.

16. Upon what terms was a treaty of peace made with Mexico?

17. What causes led to the War of Sececsion?

19. Name one great battle in each year of this war.

19. How was the Union reconstructed?

20. What important amendments were made to the Constitution?

SET VIII.

TEN QUESTIONS — TEN CREDITS EACH.

1. Mention five of the most important discoveries made between 1492 and 1550.

2. What French settlements were made within the present boundaries of the United States?

3. How did any of the country west of the Mississippi originally come into the possession of the Spanish?

4. How were Kentucky and Utah settled?

5. What portion of the United States was bought from France? When and how?

6. How was the expense of the War of the Revolution met?

7. Name one important battle in which Burgoyne was engaged; Cornwallis; Washington.

8. How long did the Mexican War continue?

9. Name two important battles of the war of Secession that were fought in Virginia; one in Pennsylvania; one in Tennessee; one in which Admiral Farragut was engaged.

10. What were the results of the War of Secession?

SET IX.

TEN QUESTIONS — TEN CREDITS EACH.

1. From what nations have we acquired Louisiana, Florida, and California?

2. Name the battles fought and two towns captured by General Taylor in Mexico.

3. What battles were fought on the west side of the Niagara River in 1814?

4. By whom and for what length of time are Senators in Congress elected?

5. When and where did the convention meet that

framed the federal Constitution, and who was its president?

6. What did Count de Rochambeau do for the Americans?

7. Give a sketch of General Greene's campaign in the Carolinas.

8. Why did the Colonies think England had no right to tax them?

9. What taxes were imposed immediately after the repeal of the Stamp Act?

10. What battles were fought in Virginia during the War of the Revolution? of 1812? Give a sketch of the last campaign in Virginia, 1865.

SET X.

TEN QUESTIONS — TEN CREDITS EACH.

1. State the causes of the "French and Indian War." Name two of the principal battles fought, the commanders on each side, and the victorious party. What territory did England gain by the war?

2. When was Jamestown settled? St. Augustine?

3. When and by whom was the Hudson River discovered? the Mississippi? the Pacific Ocean?

4. Name the chief cause of the Revolution.

5. When, where, and by whom, on the part of Americans, was the treaty of peace concluding the war signed?

6. Name one of the principal battles fought during each of the years of the Revolution, the commander on each side, and the victorious party in each.

7. When and where was negro slavery introduced into America? and when and by whom was the emancipation proclamation issued?

8. What territory was acquired by the United States during Jefferson's administration? how was it obtained?

9. State the causes of the War of 1812. Name two of the most important engagements on land and two naval battles.

10. In what battles during the War of Secession was Grant commander? Lee? Sherman?

CONSTITUTION AND GOVERNMENT OF THE UNITED STATES.

SET I.

TWENTY QUESTIONS — FIVE CREDITS EACH.

1. WHO was president of the convention which framed the Constitution of the United States, and what distinguished men were members of it?

2. Why was the adoption of such a Constitution considered necessary?

3. Why does the Constitution allow each State two Senators, but members of the House of Representatives in proportion to population?

4. Why was the Constitution so framed that Senators should be elected by the State Legislatures, and Representatives by the direct vote of the people?

5. How are the Judges of the Supreme Court of the United States elected? Why not by direct vote of the people?

6. What powers are vested in the General Government?

7. What exclusive powers have States?

8. Where must bills for raising revenue originate?

9. How can the President of the United States be impeached?

10. What is meant by Presidential Electors? How are they chosen?

11. What representation has each State in the Electoral College?

12. If the Electors fail to elect a President, and the House of Representatives also fail to elect, who would become President?

13. What Presidents have been chosen by the House of Representatives?

14. For what offices does the President have the appointing power?

15. What officers constitute the President's Cabinet?

16. Explain the manner in which a President is nominated.

17. What connection has a primary election with a national convention?

18. How can the Constitution be amended?

19. Mention any amendment made to the Constitution since its adoption.

20. Mention the last amendment. S.

SET II.

FIVE QUESTIONS — TEN CREDITS EACH.

1. What is the purpose of government?

2. What are the duties of Vice-president.

3. How often does Congress meet?

4. Mention some duties performed by the Senate in which the House of Representatives does not participate.

5. How are amendments to the Constitution made?

SET III.

TWENTY QUESTIONS — FIVE CREDITS EACH.

1. What were the colonial forms of government?

2. When, where, and why did the first Continental Congress meet?

3. When and where did the second Continental Congress meet, and what were some of its acts?

4. When were the Articles of Confederation finally ratified ?

5. What led to the formation of the present Constitution ?

6. What were some of the defects of the confederative form of government ?

7. Name the departments of our government, and the powers of each.

8. Of what does Congress consist ?

9. State the advantages of having two Houses of Congress.

10. By what officer and in what manner is the census taken ?

11. What provision is there in regard to territorial representation ?

12. Who is the presiding officer of the Senate, and why ?

13. What body has the power of impeachment, and what the power to try impeachment ?

14. What is an executive session ?

15. How many readings must a bill receive before being passed ?

16. What is a veto ?

17. How is a bill passed over a veto ?

18. What is a tariff ?

19. What qualifications must a man have to be eligible to the office of President ?

20. To be eligible to the Vice-presidency ?

SET IV.

TEN QUESTIONS—FIVE CREDITS EACH.

1. What is the purpose of a written constitution ?

2. What is the office of civil government ?

3. What is the object of separating the officers of government into independent departments ?

4. Why should a legislature consist of two bodies?

5. Why does the Constitution provide that the President shall be elected by electors chosen by the people?

6. What is the purpose of oaths of office?

7. How may the Constitution be amended?

8. How may a bill become a law, notwithstanding the veto of the President?

9. What is the object of the writ of *habeas corpus?*

10. When only can private property be taken for public use?

SET V.

FIVE QUESTIONS — FIVE CREDITS EACH.

1. When was the Constitution of the United States adopted, and who framed it?

2. What, in substance, is the Fourteenth Amendment to the Constitution? the Fifteenth?

3. In framing the Constitution, *why* were the smaller States allowed an equal representation with the larger States in the Senate?

4. In what particulars was the Constitution an improvement on the Articles of Confederation?

5. For what offices does the President have the appointing power, subject to the confirmation by the Senate?

THEORY AND PRACTICE OF TEACHING.

SET I.

FIFTEEN QUESTIONS — FIVE CREDITS EACH.

1. WHAT item should be daily recorded in school, and what monthly summary should be made?

2. What are the principal objects of a recitation?

3. What position do you prefer to have your pupils take when reciting?

4. What are the advantages and disadvantages of keeping daily class records in recitations?

5. What is your opinion of the policy of detaining children after school for the purpose of preparing neglected lessons?

6. What is your method of regulating whispering in school?

7. What are the advantages and disadvantages of the self-reporting system in regard to deportment?

8. What do you consider just punishments for truancy? for tardiness?

9. For what particular offenses would you inflict corporal punishment?

10. Mention some of the particulars in regard to manners, in which you would instruct your pupils?

11. What is the object of the study of arithmetic?

12. Who was Horace Mann, and what did he do in the cause of education?

13. What works on teaching have you ever read, and which do you consider the best?

14. Who was Pestalozzi, and what reforms in teaching did he institute?

15. What are the particular advantages of oral spelling, and of written spelling? S.

SET II.

TEN QUESTIONS — FIVE CREDITS EACH.

1. What is the difference between instruction and training, and which occupies the higher rank in the education of the young?

2. In what sense is it true that *telling* is not *training?*

3. What is meant by the "natural order" of educating the faculties?

4. What are the prominent characteristics of the Pestalozzian System of teaching?

5. State some important principles by which teachers should be guided in conducting school exercises.

6. Should the education of the intellect be regarded as of paramount importance to that of the moral and physical nature of the child? State your reasons.

7. State briefly what you would consider the best methods of training, with special reference to the cultivation of the pupil's powers of oral expression.

8. How would you commence to teach grammar to a class which had received no instruction in the science?

9. What are some of the methods of training best adapted to the culture of the moral powers?

10. State the reasons why it is better to proceed from principles to rules and formulæ, than to adopt the inverse order.

SET III.

TEN QUESTIONS—FIVE CREDITS EACH.

1. What are "Object Lessons?"

2. What class of faculties are called into exercise in the system of "Primary instruction by Object Lessons?"

3. What instruction would you give in connection with reading lessons?

4. What do you conceive to be the relative advantages of public and private schools?

5. What is the natural order of developing the intellectual faculties of a child, and what studies call into exercise the different faculties?

6. What do you conceive to be the use of the study of Arithmetic, and what relative place would you give it in school studies?

7. What general exercises would you introduce into an unclassified school?

8. What system of reward and punishment would you adopt in school?

9. Write an outline of questions in a primary object lesson on "Glass."

10. Outline of a brief moral lesson, on "Lying."

S.

SET IV.

TEN QUESTIONS—FIVE CREDITS EACH.

1. Why should the younger pupils be confined less than the older ones?

2. What is your plan of keeping your pupils at work while in school?

3. To what extent should a teacher use a text-book in hearing a lesson?

4. To what extent should the pupil be assisted in the preparation of his lessons?

5. What is the difference between teaching and talking?

6. What, in your opinion, are the more common faults of teachers in conducting recitations?

7. What are the advantages, and what the disadvantages, of the method of propounding questions to the entire class, and requesting those who think they can answer correctly, to raise the hand?

8. What are the advantages of reviewing preceding lessons?

9. Why should the head be exempt from penal violence?

10. Why should a teacher never make a remark reflecting upon the parent of a pupil?

SET V.

TEN QUESTIONS — FIVE CREDITS EACH.

1. Mention the names of four distinguished educators.

2. What classification can be made of the mental faculties, and in what order should they be developed in a child?

3. Define sensation and perception.

4. What methods could you take to secure the attention of a class?

5. What are the prevalent errors in alphabetic instruction?

6. What is the proper use of *memory* in the process of education?

7. What use would you make of text-book questions?

8. Give three methods of developing the expressive faculties.

9. By what means can the moral nature of a child be developed?

10. What is the *first* work to be done on taking a new class?

SET VI.

TEN QUESTIONS—FIVE CREDITS EACH.

1. What do you consider the aim of all educators to be?

2. What class of studies do you consider to be especially adapted to children? Give your reasons for your opinion.

3. What is the object of studying history, and how would you secure the object?

4. Define the difference between seeing and observing, and state what means you would employ to strengthen the latter habit.

5. When would you have pupils begin the study of grammar? How would you first instruct them?

6. What help does the faculty of judgment render in the process of education?

7. Is it or is it not necessary for teachers of lower grades to acquaint themselves with the higher branches of study?

8. What educational works have you read?

9. How would you teach mental arithmetic?

10. What means would you take to correct the habit of whispering in school?

NATURAL PHILOSOPHY.

SET I.

TEN QUESTIONS — FIVE CREDITS EACH.

1. WHAT is the law of attraction of gravitation? What would be the weight of a sixty-four-pound cannon ball at the distance of the moon?

2. Define specific gravity; and give the law for finding the specific gravity of a solid.

3. What is the generally received theory of light? What are the sources of light? What is the solar spectrum?

4. What are the laws which govern the reflection and the refraction of light? What is the telescope? What is the microscope?

5. How is the barometer used to ascertain the height of mountains?

6. Mention the principal laws of motion.

7. What is the principle upon which Morse's electro-magnetic telegraph is founded?

8. How is the polarity of the magnetic needle explained?

9. Who invented the steam-engine; and what distinguished men have been connected with its improvement and application?

10. What are the laws discovered by Kepler, governing the motions and distances of the planets?

S.

SET II.

TEN QUESTIONS—FIVE CREDITS EACH.

1. Give the law of the descent of falling bodies. How long would a stone be in falling five hundred feet, and what velocity would it acquire?

2. Give the method of proving the pressure of the air by Torricelli.

3. State the great law which is at the bottom of all the mechanical phenomena of liquids, and illustrate.

4. Describe the hydraulic press, and explain the principle on which it operates.

5. Explain the principle of the screw. On what does the ratio of the power to the weight depend?

6. At what rate does sound travel in air? Is there any better medium than air for transmitting sound? What is the distance of lightning when the flash is seen nine seconds before the thunder is heard?

7. Why does the simple microscope magnify?

8. What is the magnetic meridian? Does it coincide with the geographical meridian? What is the difference between them called?

9. What are electrics? What bodies are the best conductors? Who proved that lightning and the electricity produced by a frictional machine are the same?

10. On what principle or fact does the electric telegraph depend—without which messages could not be sent? S.

SET III.

FIVE QUESTIONS—FIVE CREDITS EACH.

1. How would you illustrate the impenetrability of air?

2. How was the unit of the French system of measures determined?

3. What principle does the hydrostatic bellows illustrate?

4. What are the respective advantages of "high pressure" and "low pressure" engines?

5. Mention two kinds of lenses, and state the effect of each upon rays of light transmitted through it.

SET IV.

TWENTY QUESTIONS — FIVE CREDITS EACH.

1. What are inorganic bodies?

2. What are some of the effects of heat on substances? Name substances that may have three different forms.

3. What are imponderable agents?

4. State some of the laws pertaining to gravitation.

5. What is meant by chemical attraction?

6. If a body weighs a ton at the surface of the earth, what will it weigh one mile below the surface? How much would it weigh one thousand miles above the surface?

7. How far above the surface of the earth must a body weighing two hundred pounds be placed in order that its weight shall be reduced to twenty-five pounds?

8. How far will a body fall during the fourth second of its descent, and how far will it have fallen at the end of the fifth second?

9. What is the specific gravity of a body which weighs ten pounds in the water and twelve and one half pounds in the air?

10. How many cubic feet of air would it take to weigh as much as a cubic foot of water, and how many would have the same weight as a cubic foot of gold?

11. A piece of wood and a ten-pound ball fastened together weigh nine and one half pounds in water. The wood alone weighs one pound avoirdupois in the air: What is the specific gravity of the wood?

12. State a law relative to the pressure of liquids.

13. Two bodies are moving in the air; one, weighing fifty pounds, moves at the rate of one hundred miles per hour; the other, weighing ten pounds, has a velocity of nine miles per minute. How do their momenta compare?

14. With a lever of the third kind, thirty feet long, how great a power will it require to raise a weight of one thousand two hundred pounds, the fulcrum being eight feet from the power?

15. What is the law of refracted light?

16. What is the undulatory theory of light? Give an explanation of the causes of dawn and twilight.

17. What is the law relative to the intensity of light at different distances from a luminous body?

18. What is meant by the harmony of colors?

19. State how we see.

20. State the principle on which the steam-engine is constructed.

SET V.

FIFTEEN QUESTIONS—FIVE CREDITS EACH.

1. What is the law of centrifugal force?

2. Give three laws of motion.

3. A man at the earth's surface weighs two hundred pounds—what would he weigh four thousand miles above the surface? Two thousand miles below the surface?

4. How far will a stone fall in ten seconds?

5. What is the velocity of a stone which has been falling ten seconds?

6. How far will a stone fall in the tenth second?

7. What are the principal motive powers?

8. What is meant by an engine of one-horse power?

9. What is the hydrostatic press, and on what law is its action based?

10. What is the specific gravity of gold?

11. What are the properties of air?

12. What is heat supposed to be, and how is it communicated?

13. What can you say of heat as a motive power?

14. What are the laws of reflected light?

15. What is actinism? S

PHYSIOLOGY AND HYGIENE.

SET I.

TEN QUESTIONS — FIVE CREDITS EACH.

1. How are the arteries and the veins connected?
2. What is the mucous membrane? Its office?
3. What are the ganglionic nerves, and what is their function?
4. Explain the structure of the heart.
5. What distinction is made between the functions of the cerebrum and cerebellum?
6. What are the functions of the skin.
7. What is the cause of a common cold, and what directions can you give for curing one?
8. Why should not children be required to study hard immediately after eating?
9. Why should not children study late at night?
10. Why would you teach scholars to breathe through the nostrils rather than the mouth? S.

SET II.

SEVEN QUESTIONS — FIVE CREDITS EACH.

1. (*a*) Of what are the bones composed?
   (*b*) What envelops them?
   (*c*) What hold them together?
   (*d*) How many bones in the spine?
   (*e*) How many ribs in the human body?

2. (*a*) Of what are the muscles composed?
   (*b*) By what attached?
   (*c*) To what attached?
   (*d*) By what inclosed?
   (*e*) Uses?
3. (*a*) Name the layers of the skin.
   (*b*) Functions of the skin.
   (*c*) What glands in the skin?
   (*d*) Divisions of the brain?
   (*e*) What membrane surrounds it?
4. (*a*) Names of the cavities of the heart.
   (*b*) Names of the valves of the heart.
   (*c*) What are arteries?
   (*d*) What connect the veins and arteries?
   (*e*) How does the chyle enter the blood?
5. (*a*) Function of the lymphatics.
   (*b*) Functions of the lacteals.
   (*c*) What are the chief agents of secretion in the body?
   (*d*) Of what two parts is blood composed?
   (*e*) What are the organs of respiration?
6. (*a*) What is the function of the respiratory organs?
   (*b*) Name the vocal organs.
   (*c*) Of what is the nervous system composed?
   (*d*) Into what two parts is the brain divided?
   (*e*) What are the special functions of the larger part?
7. (*a*) Name the parts of the eye.
   (*b*) Office of the iris.
   (*c*) Of what three parts is the ear composed?
   (*d* and *e*) Describe the auditory nerve. S.

SET III.

TEN QUESTIONS—TWO AND ONE HALF CREDITS EACH.

1. State the locality in the body of the patella, hyoid bone, ulna, scapula, and tibia.
2. Describe the hip joint.
3. Where is the liver, and what are its functions.
4. Name the digestive fluids.
5. What is the difference between arteries, veins, and capillaries?
6. What is the blood heat of man, and how is it believed to be maintained?
7. Mention the locality and office of the pancreas.
8. What is the normal rate of the pulse in an adult, and how does it vary in old age, infancy, fever, and debility?
9. What is the office of the lymphatics? Of the lacteals?
10. What excretory organs chiefly remove the waste carbon from the body? Which remove its waste nitrogen and salts?

SET IV.

TOTAL: TWENTY-FIVE QUESTIONS—SEVENTY-FIVE CREDITS.

Ten Questions—Two Credits Each.

1. What is physiology?
2. How many bones in the skull?
3. Where is the patella?
4. What connects the bones?
5. By means of what do we move the bones?
6. What prevents the teeth from quickly wearing out?
7. What important organ is on the left side of the body?
8. Into what does the secretion of the liver pass?

9. Through what vessels is the blood distributed over the body?

10. Through what vessels does the food pass from the intestines into the circulation?

Ten Questions — Three Credits Each.

11. What are glands?
12. What are the organs of respiration?
13. To what is the dark color of the blood owing?
14. What is the cause of animal heat?
15. What is the cuticle?
16. What is the office of the nerves?
17. What is the cerebrum?
18. Mention the coats of the eye.
19. What is the effect of closing the Eustachian tube?
20. Which of the five senses do you think the most important?

Five Questions — Five Credits Each.

21. Mention three things conducive to the health of the muscles.
22. Mention three things conducive to the health of the digestive organs.
23. Mention three things conducive to healthy circulation.
24. Mention three things promotive of healthy respiration.
25. Mention three things conducive to a healthy nervous system.

S.

SPELLING.

SET I.

ONE HUNDRED WORDS.

EXAMINERS will pronounce these words to the applicants under examination, so that there may be no mistake about the words intended.

reminis′sense	rat′efy	responsi′eble
numat′icks	im′pune′	alle′geance
super cil′yus	os′silate	compare′ative
tas′siturn	vin yet′	dellega′sion
sin′onim	in cor′regeble	pos es′ion
re treeve′	ir re sis ta ble	cor up′sion
ex aust′yun	spon ta nious	sus sep′table
ex hon′erate	fos for es′sense	lat′ti tude
ex il′errate	farina′cious	fysi′shun
caw′lyflour	pre tense′sious	res′i pee
ker′rocene	ma lish′us	pres′teej
nap′tha	in fal′lable	et′iket
dip′thong	man′agible	fi ness′
ben′efited	mar′rige ible	biv′wack
priv′elige	co-op′erative	bu′ro
sper ma cit′y	mod′dyfyed	Shakespear
dis shev′elled	embar′rasment	prit′ti ness
com plec′tion	par′alell	dayn′ty ness
rec com mend	men′tain ance	blame′able
cro shay′	explis′itly	charge′able
bru net′	exces′ivly	move′able

ter′rable
pham′flet
at tasha′
shin′yon
ap ro po′
al′cho hol
change′able
fullfill
beaf′stake
dip the′ria
bron chee′tis
diarre′a
skillfull

halle lu′ya
shar′latan
gro tesk′
sas′si frass
shap par ral′
gas con nade′
live′lyhood
moc′cazin
opake′
sponta′nious
advanta′gous
boun′ty ous
bu′ty ous

du′tey ous
loqua′shious
crit′i cize
ad′vertize
tyr′rannize
en′terprize
su′pervize
tipog′rafy
fo tog′ra fer
hem′mor rage
e fem′erral

S.

SET II.

TWENTY-FIVE WORDS — TWO CREDITS EACH.

1. Retrievable.
2. Receevable.
3. Unexpresable.
4. Unlimitly.
5. Masheen.
6. Sfericle.
7. Reccomendashun.
8. Clenlyness.
9. Pernishious.
10. Desicive.
11. Exibet.
12. Numness.
13. Cirkuit.
14. Calliko.
15. Acquited.
16. Monkies.
17. Centinels.
18. Sheeves.
19. Alegatur.
20. Liveing.
21. Disagreeable.
22. Flys.
23. Ocazionally.
24. Parigraf.
25. Cillindricall.

Twenty-five Credits.

Copy and correct the spelling, punctuation, and capitals of the following extract from Walter Scott. The spelling of the proper names is correct as printed. One credit off for each word misspelled, one off for each misplaced capital, and one for any important error in punctuation.

"have you confesed yourself Brother said the Templar Guilbert and have you heard mass this morning that you may perrill your life so frankly. i am fiter to meet death than thou art answered the Disinherited Knight for by this name the stranger had recorded himself in the book of the tourney. then take your place in the lists said de bois guilbert and take your last look upon the Sun for this night thou shalt sleep in paradise. grant mercy for thy courtesy replied the Disinhereted Knight and to requite it I advise the to take a fresh horse and a new lance for by my honor you will need both."

Geographical Names. Ten Credits.

1. Tenese.
2. Indianna.
3. Connetticut.
4. Cincinnatti.
5. Masachusets.
6. Venezwala.
7. Himmalah Mountains.
8. Reeo Janaro.
9. Bordo.
10. San deeago.

Fifteen Credits.

[One Credit off for each misspelled word and each misplaced capital.]

"Orthography treats of letters, sylabels, seperate words and speling."

"the first word of every distinct Sentence should begin with a Capital.

"the orthography of our language is atendid with much unsertinty and perplecksity."—BROWN's *Grammar.*

"Words of one sylable, and words accented on the last sylable ending with a single consonent, preseded by a single vowell doubble the final consonent on reseiving an additional terminashun beginning with a vowell: as rob, robbing; aquit, aquiting."—WILSON's *Speller.* S.

SET III.

Pronunciation.

1. Ad-ven-tish-us.
2. Ar-gil a-shus.
3. Av-er-du-poize′.
4. Hem-mer-age.
5. Fu′-she-a.
6. Ben-e-fit-ted.
7. Priv-i-lege.
8. Ban-nan′-na.
9. Gauge.
10. Men-azh′-e-re.
11. Sperm-a-city.
12. Be-le-gur.
13. Se-ta-shus.
14. Cat-ter-pil-lar.
15. Dis-shev-el-led.
16. Min-yon-et′.
17. Nap-tha.
18. Com-plec-tion.
19. Bat-tal-yun.
20. Cer-tif-i-cate.
21. Rec-com-mend.
22. Re-con′-ne-zance.
23. Law′-de-num.
24. Seige.
25. Cro′-shay.

Pronunciation.

26. Ef-fer-ves′-sence.
27. Strick′-nine.
28. Rar-i-fy.
29. Mi-razhe′.
30. Sil-lish′-ous.
31. Su-per-ceed.
32. Im-pune′.
33. Il-leg′-i-ble.
34. Hy-e-ro-glif-ic.
35. Os-sil-ate.
36. Da-ger′-re-an.
37. Cam-el-leop-ard.
38. Ex-il-ler-ate.
39. Su-per-in-tend-ent.
40. In-cor-e-gi-ble.
41. Rap-pa-han-nock.
42. Chat-ta-noo-ga.
43. Sym-me-try.
44. Vin-yet′.
45. Trys-sil-la-ble.
46. Ir-re-sis-ta-ble.
47. Koo-chook. (India-rubber.)
48. Spon-ta-ni-ous.
49. Fos-fo-res-sense.
50. In-can-des-sense.

S.

SET IV.

1. Discurigment.
2. Sitadell.
3. Campaign.
4. Infalable.
5. Politishan.
6. Recomend.
7. Dissiplin.
8. Effervessense.

9. Manigeable.
10. Despondensey.
11. Fosforessense.
12. Shampane.
13. Cooperitive.
14. Moddifyed.
15. Embarasment.
16. Reconnezance.
17. Purifyed.
18. Consilliation.
19. Rebelious.
20. Parrallell.
21. Tenasety.
22. Judgement.
23. Cirtifecates.
24. Kalibeate.
25. Disollution.
26. Belliggerant.
27. Proclaimation.
28. Maintainence.
29. Sinonim.
30. Explisitely.
31. Exsesive.
32. Necesaty.
33. Responceable.
34. Curansy.
35. Alleigeance.
36. Aprehend.
37. Judishousley.
38. Terific.
39. Compareative.
40. Farrinacious.
41. Exhonnorrate.
42. Sanguinaryly.
43. Delligation.
44. Ambullanse.
45. Clarrafy.
46. Posescion.
47. Coruption.
48. Irisponcible.
49. Schollars.
50. Susseptable. S.

SET V.

1. Dispepsy.
2. Ekwipt.
3. Parelelogramme.
4. Exchequer.
5. Tecknecle.
6. Awdassety.
7. Irrasseble.
8. Suspicion.
9. Coajjuter.
10. Machination.
11. Dynasty.
12. Escenshal,
13. Vinyet.
14. Vissera.
15. Millishy.
16. Vittels.
17. Nitch.
18. Paregoric.
19. Satellite.
20. Lezhurly.
21. Fusha.
22. Newmatticks.
23. Sikology.
24. Saccharine.

25. Sirringe.
26. Amanyuencis.
27. Impressible.
28. Dissiplin.
29. Criterion.
30. Lettis.
31. Precocity.
32. Cymbal.
33. Tyranny.
34. Haynus.
35. Fallayshus.
36. Embarrassment.
37. Sittadel.
38. Discurridgment.
39. Irresponsible.
40. Coquetry.
41. Efishent.
42. Caustic.
43. Maggasine.
44. Buisness.
45. Aristocratic.
46. Hemoridge.
47. Volubility.
48. Extraordinary.
49. Privilege.
50. Prejudis.

SET VI.

(*To be dictated by the Examiners.*)

FIFTY CREDITS.

Twenty Words — One Credit Each.

1. Satellite.
2. Gauge.
3. Diaphragm.
4. Icicle.
5. Nonpareil.
6. Michaelmas.
7. Synonym.
8. Mucilage.
9. Sieve.
10. Siege.
11. Until.
12. Welfare.
13. Permitted.
14. Duly.
15. Daily.
16. Maintenance.
17. Transferred.
18. Correspondence.
19. Accommodation.
20. Distillation.

(*Ten Credits. — One off for each misspelled word.*)

The Asiatic Governments are despotic ; the religions very diverse. Buddhism, an idolatrous worship, prevails in Thibet, China, and Japan ; Brahminism, also idolatrous, in India.

(*Ten Credits. — One off for each error.*)

To retaliate upon France and England, Congress, in December, 1807, decreed an embargo, by which all American vessels and sailors were called home and detained, and foreign vessels were prohibited from taking cargoes from our ports.

Ten Credits. — One off for each error.

The conduct of Columbus was characterized by the grandeur of his views, and the magnanimity of his spirit. Instead of ravaging the newly found countries, like many of his contemporary discoverers, who were intent only on immediate gain, he regarded them with the eyes of a legislator.

He was naturally irascible and impetuous, and keenly sensible to injury.

SET VII.

SPELLING.

lettuce	oxygen	machinate
mortise	pyrotechnic	saccharine
nuisance	malleable	epiphany
neuter	infallible	spermaceti
tortoise	supplicate	worsted
mullein	archetype	orrery
murrain	chrysalis	obsequies
zephyr	rehearse	metonymy
circuit	imburse	javelin
surfeit	tranquillity	irrigate
edible	humility	inoculate
schedule	empire	innocence
salvable	polygamy	idiosyncrasy
irascible	symptom	alpaca
indelible	gherkin	apocrypha
raspberry		

SET VIII

Correct the following, if needed.

vicksen	maskeraid	highisinth
tenayshus	billyus	cincopy
anteek	chaplensee	essplaynaad
ubikwetus	medeokur	escuchon
korpussel	kaottick	homeopathy
hiperboly	metacarpus	iresipalus
ichnuman	cochineal	harpsecord
dyacoosticks	offclide	etteket
meny	conjeneal	frontispiece
marshuness	slighness	highpockrecey
apockrifal	doedekegon	tamboreen

Write out in full.	*Abbreviate.*
G. C. B.	As if he should say.
I. H. S.	No one dissenting.
Min. Plen.	His, or Her Majesty's Ships.
Q. E. F.	Fellow of the Society of Arts.
Sec. Leg.	Unknown.

Define.

potential	hesperian	syllabus.
maxillary	corollary	reciprocity
gneiss	dynamics	homogeneous
vitreous		

SET IX.

Write sentences in which the following words shall be used appropriately:—

beleaguer	conciliatory	auxiliary
deteriorate	irrepressible	sycophant
inflammable	plentitude	mnemonics
irretrievable	plebeian	typhoon
precedent	fragile	elegy
intimidate	exigency	pneumonia
indissoluble	obeisance	

SET X.

feasible
paregorick
beneffited
inelegible
condign
edeble
malafactor
surreptitious
contraband
inocculate
erysypalas
malleable
culander
facetious

subteranean
proxemate
aquious
Hebredes
quintessence
tranquillity
benefficent
tractable
sacreficial
immutable
symetry
epaulet
jeweller

defering
analyse
nutritious
salemander
surplice
exibited
recepticle
unmistakeable
caricature
ventillated
changable
euphony
sureptiteous

SET XI.

Define and Spell.

1. Definite.
2. Vague.
3. Spherical.
4. Cylinder.
5. Opaque.
6. Molluscous.
7. Zoology.
8. Confiscation.
9. Conscription.
10. Marvelous.
11. Sovereign.
12. Notoriety.
13. Exhaustion.
14. Armament.
15. Soluble.
16. Vocation.
17. Obsolete.
18. Æsthetics.
19. Ostentation.
20. Dereliction.
21. Exonerate.
22. Secession.
23. Alliterate.
24. Obliterate.
25. Salutary.

SET XII.

Words to be defined.

1. Education.
2. Knowledge.
3. Precedent.
4. Pneumatics.
5. Aëriform.
6. Lacerate.
7. Contusion.
8. Occipital.
9. Supercilious.
10. Obstacle.
11. Taciturn.
12. Soul.
13. Diameter.
14. Chirography.
15. Dissolution.
16. Idea.
17. Intimidate.
18. Linear.
19. Beneficence.
20. Circle.
21. Contiguous.
22. Reminiscence.
23. Retrieve.
24. Synonym.
25. Definition.

SET XIII.

Definitions.

Illusion. Contravene. Pathos. Anneal. Chalybeate. Ineffable. Paradox. Exotic. Parasite. Homogeneous. Chromatics. Impalpable. Obstacle. Chimerical. Omnivorous. Animalcule. Viscid. Inevitable. Pellucid. Amanuensis.

SET XIV.

TWENTY FIVE WORDS — TWO CREDITS EACH.

Define and Spell.

1. Begining.
2. Conciencious.
3. Potencial.
4. Brazier.
5. Insendiairy.
6. Remitance.
7. Postilion.
8. Synonim.

9. Logarithems.
10. Neice.
11. Redundence.
12. Merchandize.
13. Terriffic.
14. Gregareous.
15 Privelege.
16. Inseperabillity.
17. Lamantable.
18. Annallogous.
19. Symetrical.
20. Finanseer.
21. Munny.
22. Embezlement.
23. Interogation.
24. Acheiveing.
25. Ansestor.

ALGEBRA.

SET I.

TEN QUESTIONS — FIVE CREDITS EACH.

[Let all work appear upon the paper.]

1. MULTIPLY $a^2 - 2ax - b^2 + bx$ by $b^2 + ax$.

2. Divide $3x^3 + 4abx^2 - 6a^2b^2x - 4a^3b^3$ by $2ab + x$.

3. Reduce to its simplest form $\dfrac{m^3a^2 + n^3a^2}{a(m^2+n^2) - man}$.

4. A certain fraction becomes 1 when 3 is added to the numerator, and $\frac{1}{2}$ when 2 is added to the denominator; find it.

5. Write the square of $1 + 2x - x^2 - \frac{1}{2}x^3$.

6. Simplify the fraction $\dfrac{\frac{1}{2}(x + 1\frac{2}{3}) - \frac{2}{3}(1 - \frac{3}{4}x)}{1\frac{3}{4} - \frac{1}{3}(x + 4\frac{1}{4})}$

7. Solve the following equation: $\dfrac{x}{2} - \dfrac{2x}{3} + \dfrac{3x}{4} = 11 + \dfrac{x}{8}$.

8. What two numbers are there, whose sum is 48 and difference 22?

9. A is twice as old as B; twenty-two years ago he was three times as old. Required A's present age.

10. Solve the following equations: $\begin{cases} 2x - y = 8 \\ 2y + x = 9 \end{cases}$

SET II.

TEN QUESTIONS — TEN CREDITS EACH.

1. Define coefficient, exponent, term, reciprocal, and surd; and give illustrations of each.

2. Demonstrate that $a^0 = 1$.

3. Factor $a^5m - 9am^3$.

4. What number is that from which if 91 be subtracted, $\frac{1}{3}$ of the remainder will be equal to $\frac{1}{10}$ of the number?

5. $\left.\begin{aligned} x + y - z &= 1 \\ 8x + 3y - 6z &= 1 \\ 3z - 4x - y &= 1 \end{aligned}\right\}$ To find the value of x, y, and z.

6. Find the product of $(4a^3x^{-2})^2$ and $(a^{-5}x^4)$.

7. What is the square root of $a^2b^{-2} - 10ab^{-1} + 27 - 10a^{-1}b + a^{-2}b^2$?

8. $x + 16 - 3\sqrt{x + 16} = 10$. Find the value of x.

9. $\left.\begin{aligned} x + y &= 10 \\ \sqrt{\tfrac{x}{y}} + \sqrt{\tfrac{y}{x}} &= \tfrac{5}{2} \end{aligned}\right\}$ To find the value of z and y.

10. There are three numbers in geometrical progression, whose sum is 31, and the sum of the first and last is 26; what are the numbers?

SET III.

1. Divide $a^3 + x^3$ by $a - x$.

2. Find the least common multiple of $x^3 - x$, $x^3 - 1$, and $x^3 + 1$.

3. Demonstrate the rule for transposing the terms of an equation.

4. Given $\frac{x+1}{2} + \frac{x+2}{3} = 16 - \frac{x+3}{4}$, to find the value of x.

5. Divide $462, between two persons, so that for every dime which one receives, the other may receive a dollar.

6. Mention the different methods of elimination, and give an example of each.

7. Given $\frac{4}{x} - \frac{4}{y} = 1$, and $\frac{4}{x} - \frac{2}{y} = 1\frac{1}{2}$ to find the values of x and y.

8. What is the meaning of the expression $\frac{a}{o}$? Demonstrate the propriety of that signification.

9. Find the value of the expression $(-c^2 d^{-x} m^4)^5$—.

10. Given $x^{\frac{2}{3}} + y^{\frac{2}{3}} = 3x$, and $x^{\frac{1}{3}} + y^{\frac{1}{3}} = x$, to find the values of x and y.

SET IV.

1. Multiply $a^2 - 2ax - b^2 + bx$ by $b^2 + ax$.
2. Divide $3x^3 + 4abx^2 - 6a^2b^2x - 4a^3b^3$ by $2ab + x$.
3. Reduce to its simplest form $\frac{m^3a^2 + n^3a^2}{a(m^2 + n^2) - man}$.
4. A certain fraction becomes 1 when 3 is added to the numerator, and $\frac{1}{2}$ when 2 is added to the denominator; find it.
5. Write the square of $1 + 2x - x^2 - \frac{1}{2}x^3$.
6. Simplify the fraction $\frac{\frac{1}{2}(x + 1\frac{1}{3}) - \frac{2}{3}(1 - \frac{3}{4}x)}{1\frac{3}{4} - \frac{1}{3}(x + 4\frac{1}{4})}$.
7. Solve the following equation:

$$\frac{x}{2} - \frac{2x}{3} + \frac{3x}{4} = 11 + \frac{x}{8}.$$

8. What two numbers are there, whose sum is 48 and difference 22?
9. A is twice as old as B; twenty-two years ago he was three times as old. Required A's present age.
10. Solve the following equations: $\begin{cases} 2x - y = 8 \\ 2y + x + 9 \end{cases}$

SET V.

1. From $5a^4 - 7a^3b^2 - 3c^5d^2 + 7d$ take $3a^4 - 3a^2 - 7c^5d^2 - 15a^3b^2$.

2. Multiply $3x^3 + 2x^2y^2 + 3y^2$ by $2x^3 - 3x^2y^2 + 5y^3$
3. Divide $6ax^6 + 6ax^2y^6 + 42a^2x^2$ by $ax + 5ax$.
4. Find the factors of the polynomial $a^2x - x^3$.
5. From $\frac{1 + x^2}{1 - x^2}$ take $\frac{1 - x^2}{1 + x^2}$
6. Multiply $\frac{x^4 - b^4}{x^2 + 2bx + b^2}$ by $\frac{x^2 + bx}{x - b}$.
7. Divide $1 + \frac{n - 1}{n + 1}$ by $1 - \frac{n - 1}{n + 1}$.
8. Find the values of x, y, z, in the following:—

$$\begin{cases} 2x + 4y - 3z = 22; \\ 4x - 2y + 5z = 18; \\ 6x + 7y - z = 63. \end{cases}$$

9. What is the sum of $\sqrt{18a^5b^3}$ and $\sqrt{50a^2b^3}$?

10. What two numbers are those whose sum, multiplied by the greater, is equal to 77, and whose difference, multiplied by the lesser, is equal to 12?

SET VI.

1. Define algebra.
2. Rule for algebraic subtraction; multiplication.
3. What is an equation? A quadratic equation? Rule for transportation of terms?
4. Reduce $5x + 2y = 45$, and $4x + y = 33$.
5. There is a fraction such, that if 1 be added to the numerator, its value is equal to $\frac{1}{3}$, and if 1 be added to the denominator, its value equals $\frac{1}{4}$. What fraction is it?
6. What is the 5th power of $-2a^2b^3$?
7. Square $a^{\frac{1}{2}} + b^{\frac{1}{2}}$.
8. What is the cube root of $-8a^{-6}b^{12}$?
9. Write the *surd* $a^{\frac{3}{5}}$ in as many different ways as you can.
10. Give $x^{\frac{1}{2}} - x^{\frac{1}{4}} = 2$, to find the values of x.

11. There are two numbers, one of which is greater than the other by 8, and whose product is 240. What are they?

12. What is the sum of the infinite progression $1 + \frac{1}{2} + \frac{1}{4} + \frac{1}{8}$, etc.

13. Raise $x + y$ to the 10th power.

14. Extract the cube root of $a^6 - 6a^5 + 15a^4 - 20a^3 + 15a^2 - 6a + 1$.

15. What are logarithms, and what is their use?

16. From $a - b$ subtract $c - d$, and explain the change of sign.

17. Multiply $a - b \times yc - d$, and explain.

18. Divide the number 100 into two such parts that the sum of their square roots may be equal to 14.

19. How many ways of reducing equations containing two or more unknown quantities.

20. What two numbers are those whose difference, sum, and product are as the numbers 2, 3, and 5 respectively.

SET VII.

1. $3a^2bc^2x7abcd^2 = ?$

2. $(a + b) \times (a + b) = ?$ $(a - b) \times (a - b) = ?$

3. $a^4 + 6a^2 x^2 - 4a^3x + x4 - 4ax^3 \div a^2 - 2ax + x^2 = ?$

4. Resolve $a^3 - b^3$ into its factors.

5. $\frac{a + b}{2} + \frac{a - b}{2} = ?$

6. $\frac{ax}{b - c} - \frac{ax}{b + e} = ?$

7. $x - 7 = \frac{x}{5} + \frac{x}{3}$ to find value of x.

8. Required, the square root of $2 + \sqrt{3}$.

9. At a certain election, 36,000 votes were polled, and the candidate chosen wanted but 3,000 of hav-

ing twice as many votes as his opponent. How many voted for each.

10. If A and B together can perform a piece of work in 12 days; A and C in 15 days, and B and C in 20 days. How many days will it take each person to do the work alone?

SET VIII.

1. Why do you change the signs of the subtrahend in the subtraction of polynomials?

2. Explain why the term difference does not always denote a number less than the minuend.

3. Why does multiplying a negative by a positive quantity produce a negative result?

4. What is the signification of the expression y^0, and why?

5. Express the following by positive exponents, and explain the process: $\frac{3a^{-2}b^{-1}}{6ac^{-4}}$

6. Factor $81a^4 - 16b^4$.

7. Solve the following, and give reasons for the various transformations in the process:—

$$\frac{ax-b}{4} + \frac{a}{3} = \frac{bx-a}{3}$$

8. Simplify $(a^2b^3c^2d)^6$, and $(-a^mb^nc)^4$.

9. Develop $(4a - 5d)^3$ by theorem.

10. Add $\sqrt{\frac{6}{10}}$ and $\sqrt{\frac{5}{27}}$.

11. Simplify $\sqrt{\frac{50}{588}}$.

12. What are the values of x in the equation $4x^2 + 3x + \frac{3x}{5} = -14x - 3\frac{1}{5} - 4x^2$? Give the analysis.

13. Express the values of the unknown quantity in the following, without completing the square:—

$$2x^2 - 30x + 3 = -x^2 + 3\tfrac{3}{10}x - \tfrac{3}{10}.$$

14. The two roots of an equation are 5 and $-\frac{2}{3}$: what is the equation? If the two roots are a and b, what is the equation?

15. Give an algebraic demonstration of the extraction of the square root.

16. Given: $\left.\begin{array}{l} x + \frac{1}{3}y = 14 \\ \frac{1}{3}x + \frac{1}{2}y = 11 \end{array}\right\}$ to find x and y.

17. Given: $3x + 2\sqrt{x} = \frac{1}{2}x + 176$, to find the values.

18. Express the product of $2^{\frac{1}{2}} \times 2^{\frac{1}{3}}$.

19. $\left.\begin{array}{l} 2x - y = 12 \\ x^2 + 2y = 53 \end{array}\right\}$ Find the values of x and y.

20. What two numbers are those whose difference is 3, and the difference of the cubes of which is 189?

SET IX.

1. Multiply $a^2 - 2ax - b^2 + bx$ by $b^2 + ax$
2. Divide $3x^3 + 4abx^2 - 6a^2b^2x - 4a^3b^3$ by $2ab + x$.
3. Reduce to its simplest form $\dfrac{m^3a^2 + n^3a^2}{a(m^2 + n^2) - man.}$
4. A certain fraction becomes 1 when 3 is added to the numerator, and $\frac{1}{2}$ when 2 is added to the denominator; find it.
5. Write the square of $1 + 2x - x^2 - \frac{1}{2}x^3$.
6. Simplify the fraction $\dfrac{\frac{1}{2}(x + 1\frac{1}{3}) - \frac{2}{3}(1 - \frac{3}{4}x.)}{1\frac{3}{4} - \frac{1}{3}(x + 4\frac{1}{4}).}$
7. Solve the following equation:—

$$\frac{x}{2} - \frac{2x}{3} + \frac{3x}{4} = 11 + \frac{x}{8}$$

8. What two numbers are there, whose sum is 48 and difference 22?
9. A is twice as old as B; twenty-two years ago he was three times as old. Required A's present age.

10. Solve the following equations : $\begin{cases} 2x - y = 8 \\ 2y + x = 9 \end{cases}$

SET X.

1. From $\dfrac{1+x^2}{1-x^2}$ take $\dfrac{1-x^2}{1+x^2}$.

2. Prove that $a^0 = 1$.

3. Given, $x + \dfrac{x}{2} + \dfrac{x}{3}\ 5x - 2$, to find the value of x.

4. Given $\begin{cases} x + y + z = 29. \\ x + 2y + 3z = 62. \\ \dfrac{x}{2} + \dfrac{y}{3} + \dfrac{z}{4} = 10. \end{cases}$ to find x, y, and z.

5. Find the square root of $4x^6 + 12x^5 + 5x^4 - 2x^3 + 7x^2 - 2x + 1$.

6. Add $\sqrt{72}$ and $\sqrt{128}$.

7. Divide $6\sqrt{10}$ by $3\sqrt{5}$.

8. Solve the equation $x^2 - x - 40 = 170$.

9. To what is $(x^m)^n$ equal ?

10. Demonstrate the formula for finding the sum of the terms of an arithmetical progression.

SET XI.

1. Expand by means of the binomial theorem the following : $(1 - \frac{1}{2}a)^4$ and $(x^2 + 3y^2)^5$.

2. Required the product of $\sqrt[3]{15}$ and $\sqrt[2]{10}$; divide $6\sqrt{54}$ by $3\sqrt{2}$.

3. Find the greatest common divisor of $x^3 + x - 10$ and $x^4 - 16$.

4. Given $\dfrac{1}{1-\sqrt{1-x^2}} - \dfrac{1}{1+\sqrt{1-x^2}} = \dfrac{\sqrt{3}}{x^2}$, to find x.

5. Given $x^2 + y^2 = a$, and $xy = b$, to find the values of x and y.

6. Multiply $b^{-2}\sqrt[4]{a^{-3}}$ by $a^{\frac{5}{6}}b^{\frac{1}{2}}c$. Divide $a^{\frac{m}{n}}$ by $a^{\frac{p}{q}}$.

7. Write the symbol for infinity. What is it used to represent? Write the symbol for indetermination? What does it designate? If we have more unknown quantities than equations, what will be the character of the equations, and why?

8. Find the factors of the polynomial $a^2x - x^3$. Free the fraction $\dfrac{1 + x^{-2} + y^{-2}}{1 + x^{-2} - y^{-2}}$ from negative exponents.

9. Find the $\sqrt{2\frac{13}{15}}$ to within less than 0.0001.

10. Find the sixth root of 23 to within less than 0.01.

11. Find the sum of the first n terms of the progression of odd numbers, 1, 3, 5, 7, 9.

12. Find the approximate value of x in the equation $(10)^x = 3$.

13. Whereabouts, on the line between the earth and the moon, will the attraction of the earth be 16 times the attraction of the moon? Represent the mass of the moon by c, that of the earth by b, and their distance apart by a.

14. Given $x^{\frac{3}{2}} + y^{\frac{2}{3}} = 3x$, and $x^{\frac{1}{2}} + y^{\frac{1}{3}} = x$, to find the values of x and y.

15. Find the value of 1, $\frac{3}{4}$, $\frac{9}{16}$, to infinity.

16. Convert $\dfrac{a}{a - x}$ into an infinite series.

17. Given $y^3 + 48y = 104$, to find y.

18. A root of the equation $x^4 - 25x^2 + 60x - 36 = 0$, is 3; what does the equation become when freed of this root?

COMPOSITION.

SET I.

[*Style, spelling, punctuation, and capital letters, all taken into consideration in crediting. Write at least two pages of manuscript, on any one of the following topics.*]

First Subject: "GOVERNMENT."

SUGGESTIONS: Meaning of the word. Origin and necessity of government. Show the effects of anarchy. Earliest form of government; describe it. Prevailing forms of government. Distinguishing features of monarchical, democratic, and republican forms of government. Advantages of a monarchy; of a republic. Government of the United States: its strength and its weakness. Conclusion.

Second Subject: "FRIENDSHIP."

SUGGESTIONS: What is it? Origin and necessity. Illustrations of it from ancient history; modern. Benefits of true, and evils of false friendship. How friendships should be formed. Conclusion.

Third Subject: "SOCIETY."

SUGGESTIONS: What is it? When did it begin to exist? Under what forms at first? Benefits? Effects on arts and sciences. Difference between a state of barbarism and of civilization. Evils of society. Vices. Illustrations from history.

Fourth Subject: "WAR."

SUGGESTIONS: When did war begin, and how originate? What kinds of wars? Is war justifiable? Evils of war; benefits of war. Illustrate both from history. Difference between barbarous and civilized warfare. Effect of inventions upon war. Will wars ever cease?

SET II.

1. Mention four essential properties of style.

2. Define lyric, epic, and dramatic poetry.

3. Mention three authors known for simple style. Mention three authors known for abstruse style. Mention two inventive and two sarcastic writers.

4. Define the figure employed in each of the following examples: "The English gain two hours a day by clipping words." "Wherever snow falls, there is usually civil freedom." "O Jew! an *upright* judge, a learned judge!" Give examples of metaphor.

5. Give two composition subjects adapted to primary grades, and two adapted to grammar grades.

6. Write a short composition on one of the following subjects: — A Trip to Niagara. The Day's Work. An Agricultural Life. School Discipline. Money.

SET III.

1. Define rhetoric. What mental qualities are most exercised by the study of rhetoric?

2. What is figurative language? its object? Give some examples.

3. What are barbarisms? Give examples. What property of style is violated by their use?

4. Define allegory. Mention some allegory.

5. Explain the error in the following lines:—

"I bridle in my struggling muse with pain,
That longs to launch into a bolder strain."

Mention several ways of securing variety in composition.

Write a short composition on one of the following subjects: Polar Voyages; The Books I have read; School Government; Education of Woman; Dress and the Man.

PENMANSHIP.

1. WRITE the alphabet of capital letters and of small letters; grouping letters of similar form.

2. Make the elements used in forming capital letters and the small letters.

3. Give four important rules for position, height, slope, and distance of letters.

4. How many positions at the desk in writing, and which do you prefer?

5. What drill exercises would you give to secure free movements of the fingers? Hand and wrist? Arm and forearm?

6. Whose system of penmanship do you prefer, and why?

7. How would you classify an ungraded school of fifty pupils for writing lessons?

8. How often would you have writing lessons, and how long each time?

9. At what age, and how would you have children begin to write?

10. What use do you make of a blackboard in teaching writing?

ENGLISH LANGUAGE AND LITERATURE.

1. NAME the four principal changes by which Anglo-Saxon was converted into English.

2. When, and by whom, was written language devised. Name the different systems that have been employed, and the characteristics of each.

3. Give the derivation of the word *rhetoric*, and name the principal rhetorical figures. Illustraté one of them.

4. What is taste?

5. What critics among the Ancients are respectively distinguished for delicacy and correctness of taste? Who among the Moderns?

6. Compare wit, humor, and ridicule.

7. The principal varieties of poetry, and name the greatest epic in modern English literature.

8. Draw a parallel between Washington and Napoleon.

9. In whose reign did Spenser live, and who were his contemporaries? Name his principal poem? Name five living poets in order of merit.

10. Write a letter of introduction (complete) to the Secretary of State, by name (at Washington), recommending Adam Cain to a clerkship in the State Department.

ENGLISH LITERATURE.

1. NAME some influences that affected the English language before the fourteenth century. Why is Chaucer called the father of English literature?

2. What is the Baconian system of philosophy? Why was it needed? What can you say of Bacon's style?

3. What are the chief merits of Shakespeare as a writer?

4. Who were the greatest English theological writers of the sixteenth and seventeenth centuries?

5. By whom and for what was Hudibras written? What was the character of Dryden as a writer? Name some of his works.

6. Who were the leaders in the Artificial School of writers? What can you say of Pope as a poet?

7. Who were the Essayists? What influence did they exert? For what is Addison noted? Dr. Johnson?

8. Who were the great English historians?

9. What are some of the peculiarities of Byron? of Shelley? Name some of the greatest modern novelists and journalists.

10. Why should oratory flourish in a republic? What Americans have excelled as orators? as historians?

PART II.

WRITTEN EXAMINATION

FOR

GRAMMAR SCHOOLS.

CONTAINING ONE HUNDRED SETS AND TWELVE HUNDRED QUESTIONS.

ARITHMETIC.

FIRST GRADE.

SET I.

[NOTE. — No credits allowed, unless both answer and method are correct.]

TOTAL: SIXTEEN QUESTIONS — FORTY-SIX CREDITS.

Ten Questions — Two Credits Each.

1. DIVIDE 24 by $\frac{3}{8}$ and write the reasons of the operation.

2. Multiply five-ninths by four-sevenths and write a full analytical explanation of the operation.

3. In multiplying .02 by .02 explain the reason why you point off four decimal places in the product.

4. Divide $125 by 2.5.

5. Multiply the decimal twenty-five ten-thousandths by 2.5 and divide the product by five thousandths.

6. Divide .25 by $\frac{1}{3}$.

7. Divide 71 miles, 237 rods, 3 yards, 1 foot, 6 inches by 9.

8. Is the following proportion correct or incorrect? Why or why not? 10 : 5 : : 6 : 12.

9. Interest of $1,275 from January 9th, 1871 to May 7th, 1871, at 12 per cent. a year.

10. Compound interest of $150 from January 10th, 1871, to May 25th, 1871, at 2 per cent. a month.

Five Questions—Four Credits Each.

11. A boy bought apples at the rate of 5 for 4 cents, and sold them at the rate of 4 for 5 cents; what per cent. did he gain?

12. The floor of a square room measures 625 square feet; how far is it from one corner on the floor to the corner on the floor diagonally opposite, provided the floor is carpeted with carpeting one yard wide.

13. Bank discount of $500 for 2 months and 7 days at 8 per cent. a year.

14. A commission merchant received $157.75 for selling flour; his commission being 2½ per cent. how much did the flour sell for?

Two Questions—Five Credits Each.

[Partial credits allowed if the answer does not vary more than one dollar from the correct result.]

15. A mechanic contracted to work a year for $50 a month, his wages payable at the end of each month. Nothing was paid him till the close of the year, when he received the whole amount with 12 per cent. interest a year. How much did he receive?

16. On the 10th of July, 1868, John Brown, of San Francisco, hired of Henry Smith, of the same place, $2,000 in gold coin, agreeing to pay him interest at the rate of one and one half per cent. a month. On the 7th of August, 1870, John Brown paid to the holder of the note $700. What was due on the note at the time of settlement, May 15th, 1871? Put this transaction into business form and give the answer. S.

SET II.

FIFTEEN QUESTIONS—FIVE CREDITS EACH.

1. Find the greatest common divisor of 34, 306, 51, and 2,142.

2. Find the least common denominator of $\frac{1}{5}$, $\frac{1}{11}$, $\frac{1}{15}$, and $\frac{1}{205}$.

3. Two and two-thirds times one-third of a number exceeds one and three-fourths times one-half of the same number by 36,000. What is the number?

4. What sum of money must be put at interest at 4 per cent. to produce the same amount as will be produced by $1,000 loaned at 6 per cent. for the same time?

5. If the property of a city be valued at $250,000,000, and a tax of $4,000,000 be levied, what tax must a man pay whose property is valued at $15,000?

6. What will it cost to fill to the depth of 3 feet, a lot 24 feet by 132 feet, at 50 cents per cubic yard?

7. How many cords of wood in a pile 100 feet long, 60 feet wide, and 16 feet high?

8. How many seconds in the month of June?

9. What is the longest straight line that can be drawn upon the floor of a hall 60 feet wide by 80 feet ong?

10. I buy 6 apples at the rate of 3 for 5 cents, and 14 apples at the rate of 2 for 3 cents, and sell the same at the rate of 5 for 8 cents. Do I gain or lose, and how much?

11. Add $\frac{1}{2}$, $\frac{1}{5}$ and $\frac{1}{80}$, decimally.

12. Find square root of $\frac{3}{4} \times 10\frac{2}{3}$.

13. Write out analysis of the following: $\frac{3}{4}$ of 24 is how many fifths of 30?

14. If by selling property for $6,000, I lose 25 per cent., what should I have sold it for if I had gained 20 per cent.?

15. I sell property for $16,000 which cost me 3 years ago $12,000, money being worth 12 per cent. per annum, have I gained or lost, and how much?

SET III.

TWENTY QUESTIONS—FIVE CREDITS EACH.

1. In 8,421, the figure 4 expresses how many times as much as the figure 2?

2. In multiplying 1,728 by 1,836, what denomination is obtained when the 7 is multiplied by 3?

3. In subtracting 1,296 from 1,728, show why your process *ought* to give the true remainder.

4. In multiplying $\frac{3}{28}$ by 7, which is the best way? and why?

5. In dividing $\frac{3}{28}$ by $\frac{3}{7}$, how many times as often will $\frac{3}{7}$ be contained as three units? and why?

6. If $\frac{6}{7}$ of a ship cost $30,000, what will $\frac{4}{5}$ of $\frac{25}{28}$ of it cost at the same rate?

7. Received $13.28 interest on $125 at 6 per cent. How long was the money at interest?

8. Why should dividing the numerator of a proper fraction by its denominator give the quotient in a decimal?

9. Is the expression $3:6=5:8$ a true proportion? Why?

10. Correct the following: $10:5=6:12$, by changing the first term.

11. What is the value in paper of 6 months' interest on a $500 bond, the interest payable in gold at 6 per cent. a year, and the premium on gold at 12 per cent.

12. Cast the compound interest of $1,000, for 1 year and 6 months, at 8 per cent. a year but compounded semi-annually.

13. What per cent. do I make on money invested in stock at $80 a share, whose par value is $100, and dividends 6 per cent. on the par value.

14. What per cent. do I make on money invested in stock at $140 a share, whose par value is $100, and dividends 10 per cent. on the par value?

15. In extracting the square root of 49,729, why do you obtain your first figure from the 4, rather than the 49?

16. In extracting the cube root of a decimal, the first figure in the root must come from what denomination? and why?

17. Extract the square root of 144; also of .144.

18. Reduce $\frac{1}{1320}$ of a mile to yards, by one expression and cancelling.

19. How could you prove your answers to problem 17 correct, or otherwise?

20. Describe the manner you would determine the number of cords in a load of wood, the dimensions being given in feet.

SET IV.

TWENTY QUESTIONS — FIVE CREDITS EACH.

1. There are two numbers, the greater of which is 73 times 109, and their difference is 17 times 28; what is the less number?

2. What is the greatest common divisor of 32, 80, and 256?

3. What is the common multiple of 21, 35, and 42?

4. Reduce $\frac{25}{30}$, $\frac{2}{3}$, and $\frac{1}{2}$ to fractions whose denominators are 6.

5. Add $\frac{42}{140}$, $\frac{9}{70}$, $\frac{7}{28}$, and $\frac{1}{14}$.

6. What fraction added to $\frac{11}{12}$, will make $\frac{19}{20}$?

7. Multiply $\frac{8}{15}$ of $\frac{1}{24}$ by $\frac{1}{5}$ of $7\frac{1}{3}$.

8. If nine men consume $\frac{3}{4}$ of $9\frac{3}{5}$ pounds of meat in a day, how much does each man consume?

9. A boy lost $\frac{1}{2}$ of his kite string, and then added

30 feet, when it was just $\frac{4}{5}$ of its ordinary length. What was its length at first? Give analysis.

10. Read the decimal .0010404.

11. Write five hundred tenths of millionths.

12. Reduce 1.6 to a common fraction.

13. How many times will .5 of 1.75 be contained in .25 of $17\frac{1}{2}$?

14. What part of 2 rods is 4 yards $1\frac{1}{2}$ feet?

15. 16 is 15 per cent. of what number?

16. If I sell $\frac{1}{3}$ of an article for $\frac{1}{2}$ of its cost, what per cent. do I gain?

17. What is the interest of $500 for 2 years 2 months and 2 days, at 10 per cent. a year?

18. What is the present worth of $200, payable in 2 years, at 1 per cent. per month? Give analysis.

19. If a man travel 120 miles in 3 days, when the days are 12 hours long, how many days of 10 hours each will he require to travel 360 miles?

20. If a hall 36 feet long and 9 feet wide require 36 yards of carpeting, 1 yard wide, to cover the floor. how many yards $1\frac{1}{4}$ yards wide will cover a floor 60 feet long and 27 wide, if the carpet is $\frac{1}{4}$ of an inch thick?

SET V.

TWENTY QUESTIONS — FIVE CREDITS EACH.

1. Find the greatest common divisor of 246 and 372, by factoring the numbers.

2. Find the least common multiple of 246 and 372.

3. Multiply $\frac{7}{8}$ by $\frac{9}{10}$.

4 Divide $\frac{3}{4}$ by $\frac{6}{7}$.

5. Reduce $\frac{3}{4}$ and $\frac{5}{6}$ to fractions, having 60 for a common denominator.

6. Multiply four thousandths by three ten-millionths.

7. Add $\frac{3}{5}$ and $\frac{7}{8}$, and express the result in decimals.

8. A man divides his farm of $214\frac{1}{4}$ acres equally among his 9 sons; how much do each receive?

9. Reduce $\frac{3}{4}$ of a mile to lower denominations.

10. Why cannot the numbers 3, 4, 5, 6, constitute a proportion?

11. A hawk, 40 rods behind a blackbird, is following at the rate of 10 rods a minute, while the blackbird is flying at the rate of 6 rods a minute; in what time will the hawk overtake the blackbird?

12. What is the bank discount on a note for $500, payable in 2 months and 10 days, interest being $1\frac{1}{4}$ per cent. per month?

13. How long must $500 be at interest, to gain $120, at 6 yer cent. a year?

14. If I lose 20 per cent. by selling cloth at $4; what should I lose by selling at $4.50?

15. A owes B, $19; $5 of which is to be paid in 6 months, $6 in 7 months, and $8 in 10 months; what is the average time of paying the whole?

16. How many bricks, 8 inches square and 3 inches thick, will be required to cover a pavement 20 feet long, and 10 feet wide?

17. When greenbacks, measured in gold, are at 20 per cent. discount, what is gold, measured in greenbacks?

18. A, B, and C can do a piece of work in 12 days, C can do it in 24 days; A can do it in 34 days; in what time can B do it alone?

19. 20 per cent. of $\frac{4}{5}$ of a number, is how many per cent. of 2 times $\frac{3}{4}$ of $4\frac{1}{2}$ times the number?

20. If a boy buys peaches at the rate of 5 for 2 cents, and sells them at the rate of 4 for 3 cents, how many must he buy and sell, to gain $4.20?

SET VI.

TEN QUESTIONS — FIVE CREDITS EACH.

1. From $\frac{7}{8}$ of $\frac{4}{5}$ of a week, take 1 day and $2\frac{1}{2}$ hours.

2. Reduce 2 feet 6 inches to the decimal of a yard.

3. What cost $40\frac{1}{2}$ cwt. sugar, at $12\frac{1}{2}$ cents a pound?

4. At $7.50 per thousand, what will 3,132 bricks cost?

5. I send my agent $1,200 to be invested after deducting his commission of 10 per cent. What is his commission?

6. What is the interest of one dollar at 6 per cent. for 13 months and 19 days?

7. What sum must be invested at 6 per cent. to produce $1,200 per annum?

8. Present worth and discount of $375, payable in 10 months, when money is worth 2 per cent. a month?

9. Bought cloth for $$1.12\frac{1}{2}$ per yard, and sold it for $$1.06\frac{1}{4}$ per yard. What per cent. did I lose?

10. Bought a horse and cow for $173, the horse cost $93 more than the cow, what was the cost of each?

SET VII.

TOTAL: TWENTY-FIVE QUESTIONS — ONE HUNDRED CREDITS.

Ten Questions — Three Credits Each.

1. Divide 40 by $\frac{2}{3}$, and multiply the quotient by $\frac{3}{4}$.

2. Multiply 1.2 by .012, and divide the product by .6.

3. Add $\frac{3}{24}$, $\frac{5}{18}$, $\frac{2}{3}$, and $\frac{5}{12}$, and from the sum subtract $\frac{11}{15}$.

4. From $1,725\frac{1}{4}$ take $836\frac{2}{3}$.

5. Divide $4\frac{1}{3}$ by $4\frac{1}{2}$, and multiply the quotient by $\frac{5}{6}$

6. Greatest common divisor of 49, 63, 84, 91?

7. What will $25\frac{1}{2}$ pounds of tea cost at $87\frac{1}{2}$ cents a pound?

8. Multiply $\frac{3}{16}$ by .125.

9. Divide .1 by .002, and multiply the quotient by $\frac{2}{3}$.

10. From 10 cubic yards, take 2 cubic feet.

Ten Questions — Four Credits Each.

11. A building lot contains 3,300 square feet; it is $137\frac{1}{2}$ feet in length. How wide is it?

12. How many yards of carpeting one yard wide, will it take to carpet a room $28\frac{1}{2}$ feet long by 30 feet wide?

13. How many cubic inches in a box 8 feet long, 5 feet wide, and 3 feet high?

14. What will $\frac{4}{5}$ of a ton of sugar cost at 10 cents a pound?

15. Divide 33 gallons, 2 quarts, 1 pint and 3 gills by 5.

16. What will 3,550 pounds of hay cost at $1.25 a hundred weight?

17. How many grains in 25 pounds of gold?

18. How much will it cost to remove a quantity of sand 100 feet long, 25 feet wide, and 5 feet deep, at 5 cents a cubic yard?

19. In $\frac{7}{12}$ of a mile how many rods, feet, and inches?

20. If $\frac{2}{3}$ of a yard of silk cost $4\frac{1}{5}$ dollars, how much will $\frac{3}{4}$ of a yard cost?

Five Questions — Six Credits Each.

21. What is the interest of $450 for 2 years, 6 months and 15 days, at 1 per cent. a month?

22. A school numbers 800 pupils, and $12\frac{1}{2}$ per cent. of them are absent: how many are present?

23. What is 50 per cent. of $\frac{3}{8}$?

24. Suppose you hire of Henry Smith $1,000 on the 25th of May, 1869, and agree to pay him interest at the rate of $1\frac{1}{4}$ per cent. a month: write a promissory note for it.

25. Find what will be due on this note on the 15th of August, 1869. S.

SET VIII.

TEN QUESTIONS—FIVE CREDITS EACH.

1. Explain the following terms: A concrete number; ratio; present worth; bankruptcy; exchange.

2. (*a*) Explain, by an example, the process of subtraction when any figures of the subtrahend are greater than the corresponding figures of the minuend.

(*b*) Explain the method for finding the difference in time between two places when the longitude of each is known.

3. A man bought 1,000 bushels of wheat for $1,250. He finds 15 per cent. of it worthless. For how much must he sell the remainder, per bushel, so as to gain 20 per cent. upon the cost?

4. What per cent. of 75 is 15 per cent. of 175?

5. Three boys purchased a horse together. William gave $20; James 40 per cent. more than William; and George $12\frac{1}{2}$ per cent. less than both the others. What fractional part of the horse does each own?

6. Divide 32.22 by 10; divide the quotient by 100; multiply this quotient by 10; multiply this product by 1,000; multiply this product by 1; add the five results.

7. Bought a sack of coffee containing 144 pounds, at $33\frac{1}{3}$ cents a pound; I paid $2\frac{1}{2}$ cents a pound for roasting it. Allowing for a loss of $\frac{1}{32}$ in weight by roasting, at what price per pound must I sell it to gain a sum equal to $\frac{1}{4}$ of what I gave?

8. What is the difference between the simple and the compound interest of $5,425, for 4 years, at 6 per cent.?

9. What is the shortest distance that is an exact number of times a 1 foot measure, a 2 foot measure, a yard stick, and a 10 foot pole?

10. A wall which was to be built 32 feet high, was raised 8 feet by 6 men in 12 days; how many men must be employed to build the remainder of the wall in 9 days?

SET IX.

TEN QUESTIONS—FIVE CREDITS EACH.

1. What is the least common multiple of 8, 16, 24, 32, 48?

2. If $4\frac{1}{3}$ yards of silk are worth $30\frac{1}{5}$ yards of cotton, how many yards of silk would $40\frac{1}{2}$ yards of cotton be worth?

3. A grocer buys butter at $18\frac{3}{4}$ cents a pound, and sells the same at $23\frac{3}{4}$ cents a pound; what per cent. profit does he make?

4. What is the interest of $376.40, for 7 months and 3 days?

5. A merchant buys goods for $475.60, and after keeping them on hand 7 months sells the same for $560.80; what per cent. profit does he make?

6. For what sum must a note be written in order to receive from a bank $540 for 60 days?

7. What sum must be insured on $5,000, to include the premium of $2\frac{1}{8}$ per cent., and a commission of $\frac{1}{4}$ per cent. on the property insured?

8. A man bought a watch for \$75 and sold it for 20 per cent. more than it cost, which was 15 per cent. less than he asked for it; what did he ask?

9. Divide \$1,476 between A, B, and C, in such a manner that as often as A receives $\frac{1}{2}$ of a dollar B receives $\frac{3}{4}$ of a dollar and C $\frac{4}{5}$ of a dollar.

10. Cube root of 1,728.

SET X.

TEN QUESTIONS—FIVE CREDITS EACH.

1. What are the prime factors of 630? Write two composite numbers which are prime to each other.

2. From two million five thousand and sixty-four, take thirty-seven thousand two hundred and eighty-six and seventy-five thousandths. Divide the remainder by five ten-thousandths.

3. In what two ways can you multiply $\frac{7}{8}$ by 3? Show *why* the fraction is multiplied in each case.

4. If a man travel 60 miles in 7 days, how far will he travel in 1 day? Carry out the result to the lowest denomination.

5. If by selling lamps at 40 cents each, I lose 20 per cent., what per cent. shall I gain by selling them at \$9.00 per dozen? Analyze.

6. What is the equated time for paying \$100 due in 5 months, \$70 due in 4 months, and \$50 due in 2 months—all dated June 4th, 1870?

7. 15 per cent. of 484 is $33\frac{1}{3}$ per cent. of what?

8. At what rate per cent. must I invest \$600 that in 2 years and 6 months it may amount to \$705?

9. In payment for a horse I received a note for \$140 due in 1 year, 4 months, 24 days, which I immediately had discounted at a bank, at 10 per cent.: what did I in reality receive for the horse?

10. John lives 117 rods north of A, and the schoolhouse is 156 rods east of the same point: what is the shortest distance from John's house to the schoolhouse?

SET XI.

MENTAL ARITHMETIC.

1. $\frac{8}{12}$ of 48 is $\frac{1}{4}$ of what number?
2. $\frac{4}{7}$ of A's age is $\frac{4}{5}$ of B's. and 3 times B's is $\frac{5}{2}$ of C's; how old are A and B, if C is 24 years old.
3. If a man travels 9 miles in $2\frac{1}{2}$ hours, how far will he travel in $17\frac{1}{2}$ hours?
4. Add $\frac{1}{3}$, $\frac{2}{27}$, $\frac{5}{18}$, $\frac{6}{54}$, and $\frac{1}{36}$.
5. If the wages of 4 men for 8 days are $32, what will be the wages of 6 men for $5\frac{1}{2}$ days?
6. Divide 81 into two such parts that $\frac{2}{7}$ of the larger shall equal the smaller.
7. Add to a number itself, half of itself, $\frac{1}{8}$ of itself, and the result will be $2\frac{5}{8}$ the number, what is the number?
8. 15 per cent. of 60 is what per cent. of 18.
9. $\frac{1}{4}$ of a certain number is equal to $\frac{1}{2}$ of another, and their sum is 24, what are the numbers?
10. What is the interest of $60 for 2 years, 2 months and 3 days, at 8 per cent.?

SET XII.

MENTAL ARITHMETIC.

1. A boy gave away $\frac{2}{5}$ of his money to one companion, $\frac{5}{6}$ of the remainder to another, when he had 5 cents left; how much had he at first?
2. A can do a piece of work in 4 days, B can do it in 6 days, C in 8 days. In what time can A and B do it? And in what time can they all together do it?

3. If $\frac{1}{6}$ of the amount received for goods be gain, what is the gain per cent ?

4. A merchant sold $\frac{1}{3}$ of his goods at an advance of 10 per cent., $\frac{1}{4}$ of them at an advance of 15 per cent., and $\frac{1}{5}$ at a loss of 20 per cent. ; how must he sell the remainder to gain 12 per cent. on the whole ?

5. Required the time when $\frac{2}{3}$ of the time past noon is $\frac{4}{5}$ of the time past midnight.

6. A spent $\frac{1}{5}$ of his money and lost $\frac{1}{4}$ of what he had left ; he gave away $\frac{1}{6}$ of the remainder, when he had $20 left ; how much had he at first ?

7. When gold is 15 per cent. premium, how much is $100 in currency worth in gold ?

8. An agent collects an account amounting to $1,236, and is allowed 3 per cent. for collection ; how much money must he remit to his employer, and how much must he retain for his services ?

9. What must be asked for goods which cost $100, that 20 per cent. may be gained on the cost, and yet a reduction of 10 per cent. be made from the asking price ?

10. Cube root of 4,267,584.

SET XIII.

MENTAL ARITHMETIC.

1. A trader buys sugar at 10 cents a pound ; at what price per pound must he sell it to gain 20 per cent. ?

2. A grocer sells sugar at 8 cents a pound, which is $12\frac{1}{2}$ per cent. more than it cost ; what did the sugar cost a pound ?

3. If $\frac{3}{4}$ of the sum received for goods is gain, what is the gain per cent. ?

4. If 12 per cent. is gained in selling flour at $10 a barrel, what did the flour cost a barrel ?

5. The diagonal of a square field is 20 rods; what is the area of the field?

6. When gold is sold at a premium of $10\frac{7}{8}$ per cent. how much can be bought for \$50 in currency?

7. A man spent $\frac{1}{5}$ of his money and lost $\frac{1}{4}$ of the remainder; he then gave away $\frac{1}{3}$ of what he had left, and found that he had \$64 remaining; how much had he at first?

8. If a merchant gains 10 per cent. on the sale of 30 per cent. of his goods, and loses 8 per cent. on 20 per cent. of his goods, how must he sell the remainder to gain 15 per cent. on the whole?

9. If goods are bought at $\frac{3}{4}$ of their value, and sold for 10 per cent. more than their value, what is the gain per cent.?

10. A man being asked the hour, said that $\frac{1}{3}$ of the time to midnight was equal to $\frac{5}{6}$ of the time to noon. What was the hour?

SET XIV.

MENTAL ARITHMETIC.

1. If a bushel of corn cost $\frac{5}{6}$ of a dollar, how many bushels can be bought for $\$11\frac{2}{3}$?

2. How many pounds of sugar, at $6\frac{1}{4}$ cents a pound, can be bought for \$20?

3. A farmer sold $\frac{3}{5}$ of a flock of sheep to one man, and $\frac{3}{4}$ of the remainder to another, when he found he had 10 sheep left; how many sheep were there in the flock at first, and how many did he sell at each time?

4. What is the number, to which if we add its fourth and its fifth, the sum will be 58?

5. What is the number, to which if we add itself, its half, its third, its fifth, its sixth, one fourth of the sum will be 48?

6. A farmer sells hay at $16 a ton, which is $\frac{4}{5}$ of the cost: what is the cost, and how much does he gain per cent.?

7. A person being asked the time of day, said that the time past noon was equal to $\frac{4}{5}$ of the time to midnight; what was the time?

8. A man bought a horse and chaise and harness for $360. He paid $\frac{2}{3}$ as much for the horse as for the chaise, and $\frac{1}{2}$ as much for the harness as for the horse; how much did he pay for each?

9. A boy being asked his age, answered that if $\frac{4}{5}$ of his age and 3 years were added to his age, the sum would be 30 years; what was his age?

10. James said his purse and money were worth $27, but his purse was worth $\frac{1}{8}$ of his money; how much money had he in his purse?

ARITHMETIC.

SECOND GRADE.

SET I.

[NOTE.—No credits whatever allowed, unless both answer and method are correct.]

TOTAL : SEVENTEEN QUESTIONS—FIFTY CREDITS.

Ten Questions—Two Credits Each.

1. MULTIPLY five sevenths by two thirds, and write out an analytical solution.

2. Divide 6 by $\frac{2}{3}$, and explain the reason of the operation.

3. Multiply the decimal twelve thousandths by twelve hundredths, and divide the product by .0006.

4. Divide $1.44 by 1.2.

5. Multiply $2\frac{1}{4}$ by $4\frac{1}{2}$, and divide the product by 1.25.

6. Greatest common divisor of 96, 120, 168.

7. Add five twelfths, four ninths, seven fifteenths, three eighths.

8. What is $\frac{1}{2}$ of 1 year, 5 months, 3 weeks, 5 days, 3 minutes, and 5 seconds?

9. In $\frac{5}{7}$ of a mile, how many rods, feet, and inches?

10. What will 45,675 pounds of wheat cost, at $1.75 per hundred?

Five Questions—Four Credits Each.

11. What per cent. of 4 is 5?

12. Write a promissory note.

13. Interest of $425.75 from January 15, 1870, to May 14th, 1871, at 10 per cent. a year.

14. Interest of $150 from December 15th, 1870, to May 15th, 1871, at $1\frac{1}{4}$ per cent. a month.

15. What is the exact number of geographical miles in the circumference of the earth?

Two Questions—Five Credits Each.

16. How many pickets, each 3 inches wide, placed 3 inches apart, will it take to fence round a lot 4×10 rods?

17. A cubic foot of water weighs 62 pounds 8 ounces. What is the pressure on one square rod at the bottom of the sea, where the water is 1,000 fathoms deep?

S.

SET II.

TEN QUESTIONS—FIVE CREDITS EACH.

1. What is a prime number? Illustrate.
   What is a multiple? Illustrate.

2. If $\frac{4}{5}$ of a bushel of wheat cost $\$\frac{3}{4}$, what will $5\frac{1}{3}$ bushels cost?

3. A horse and carriage are worth $320; the horse is worth $\frac{2}{3}$ as much as the carriage; what is the value of each?

4. Divide .003 by .24. Also divide .24 by .003.

5. How many bushels of corn, at $.75 a bushel, will pay for a pile of wood 12 feet long, 12 feet high and 4 feet wide, at $9 a cord?

6. A certain number plus 75 per cent. of itself, is 147; what is the number?

7. A real estate agent sold a lot $37\frac{1}{2}$ feet front, at $70 a foot; what was his commission at $2\frac{1}{2}$ per cent.?

8. 3 pecks, 4 quarts is what decimal of a bushel?

9. What is the value of the following fraction:

$$\left\{\frac{3\frac{1}{4}}{8\frac{1}{3}} \times \frac{1\frac{1}{3}}{5}\right\} \div \frac{1}{6}?$$

10. Find the product of .875, .025, and .0006.

SET III.

FIFTEEN QUESTIONS—FIVE CREDITS EACH.

1. Write in figures two hundred and forty, and one thousand three hundred seventy-six hundred-thousandths.

2. Express in Roman notation the number 1,859.

3. Multiply 7,030 by 164,000 by the shortest method.

4. Add $\frac{2}{3}$, $\frac{5}{6}$ and $\frac{3}{8}$.

5. From $7\frac{1}{2}$ take $3\frac{5}{9}$.

6. Two persons start from the same point at the same time, and travel in the same direction; one travels at the rate of 28 miles a day, the other at the rate of 37 miles a day; how far apart will they be in 6 days?

7. Divide $\frac{11}{15}$ by $\frac{1}{7}$ of $\frac{2}{3}$.

8. If $\frac{5}{6}$ of a ton of hay can be bought for $15, what part of a ton can be bought for $1?

9. Multiply twenty-three hundredths by nine thousandths.

10. Divide nine hundred and ninety-two ten-thousandths by thirty-two hundreths.

11. A man bought a farm containing 125 acres, for $2,922.50; for how much must he sell it per acre to gain $500?

12. Reduce $\frac{1}{3}$, $\frac{3}{5}$, and $\frac{4}{7}$ to a common denominator.

13. What is the interest of $376 for 8 months and 20 days, at 10 per cent. a year?

14. At 11 cents a pound, what will be the cost of 3 cwt. of coffee?

15. From ten thousand take ten thousandths.

S.

SET IV.

MENTAL ARITHMETIC.

Ten Questions — Five Credits Each.

1. 21 is $\frac{7}{10}$ of how many times 8?

2. A man sold a watch for $63, which was $\frac{7}{5}$ of what it cost him; how much did he gain by the bargain?

3. A ship's crew have provisions sufficient to last 3 men 10 months; how long would it last 5 men?

4. $\frac{4}{7}$ of 63 is $\frac{6}{5}$ of how many times 8?

5. $\frac{3}{8}$ of 64 is $\frac{6}{10}$ of how many sixths of 30?

6. If 3 men can do a piece of work in 7 days, how long would it take 4 men to do it?

7. A man sold a piece of cloth for $42, by which bargain he lost $\frac{2}{9}$ of what the cloth cost him. How much did it cost him, and how much did he lose?

8. A man sold 9 yards of cloth for $$7\frac{2}{3}$ a yard, and received 8 firkins of butter, at $$6\frac{3}{4}$ a firkin; how much was then due him?

9. How many three-cent pieces will it take to make $10.00?

10. How many pounds of beefsteak at $12\frac{1}{2}$ cents a pound can be bought for $5.00?

SET V.

MENTAL ARITHMETIC.

Ten Questions — Five Credits Each.

1. How much sugar, that is worth $8 a hundred weight, can be bought for 4 cords of wood, at $7 a cord?

2. If a man receives $5 for 3 days' work, how many shillings is that a day?

3. $\frac{7}{8}$ of 60 are how many times 8?

4. If 3 men can do a piece of work in 12 days, in how many days will 4 men do the same work?

5. If a staff 3 feet long, cast a shadow of 2 feet at 12 o'clock, what is the length of a pole that casts a shadow 18 feet at the same time of day?

6. A ship's crew have provision sufficient to last 3 men 10 months; how long will it last 5 men?

7. $\frac{4}{5}$ of 15 are $\frac{6}{10}$ of what number?

8. If a cask of wine costs $48, what are $\frac{5}{8}$ of it worth?

9. Bought 20 pears at the rate of 2 for 3 cents, how much did they come to?

10. At 20 cents a pound, how many pounds of coffee can be bought for $15.00?

SET VI.

MENTAL ARITHMETIC.

Ten Questions—Five Credits Each.

1. If $\frac{2}{3}$ of $\frac{3}{5}$ of a number be subtracted from $\frac{3}{4}$ of six times the number, the remainder will be 4; what is the number?

2. If $\frac{3}{5}$ of a barrel of flour cost $$6\frac{3}{5}$, how many barrels can be had for $$104\frac{1}{2}$?

3. If 4 men do a piece of work in 9 days, in how many days will 3 men do a piece of work $\frac{1}{4}$ as large?

4. After spending $5 less than $\frac{1}{2}$ of my money, I have $\frac{3}{5}$ left. How much had I at first?

5. $\frac{2}{3}$ of 5 is $\frac{5}{8}$ of how many times $\frac{3}{4}$?

6. A cistern containing 70 gallons is emptied by two pipes in 7 hours; one pipe alone will empty it in $8\frac{3}{4}$ hours, in what time will the other empty it when it is $\frac{3}{5}$ full?

7. Paid $30 for 7 pieces of cloth, each containing 10 yards. Required cost of each yard and each piece?

8. Gave 13 cents for apples at the rate of 6 for $2\frac{1}{6}$ cents. How many did I get?

9. How often is $3\frac{4}{7}$ contained in $\frac{2}{3}$?

10. If 1 peach is worth 3 apples, and 9 apples are worth 1 orange, how many oranges can you get for 54 apples and 18 peaches?

SET VII.

MENTAL ARITHMETIC.

Ten Questions—Five Credits Each.

1. If 2 apples cost 4 cents, what would 4 apples cost?

2. How many dozen eggs, at 25 cents a dozen, must you give for 100 pounds of sugar at 25 cents a pound?

3. How many eggs, at the rate of 3 for 10 cents, can you buy for $5.00?

4. If 4 yards of silk cost $12, what will 40 yards cost?

5. A man had 360 dollars and gave $\frac{5}{6}$ of them away, how many of them did he have left?

6. If one yard of cloth cost $\$\frac{3}{4}$, how much will 50 yards cost?

7. If 4 pounds of butter cost $1.20, what will 150 pounds cost?

8. If 8 barrels of apples cost $36, what will 100 barrels cost?

9. At 1 cent a pound, how many barrels of potatoes can be bought for $40?

10. In 3,427 cents, how many dollars?

ARITHMETIC.

THIRD GRADE.

SET I.

TOTAL: TWENTY-FIVE QUESTIONS — ONE HUNDRED CREDITS.

Ten Questions — Three Credits Each.

1. WRITE 1779 in Roman numerals.
2. In 20 rods, 12 feet, 9 inches, how many inches?
3. How many cubic inches in 25 cubic feet
4. Add $\frac{2}{5}$ and $\frac{7}{10}$.
5. Divide $4\frac{1}{2}$ by $1\frac{2}{3}$, and divide the quotient by 9.
6. Multiply $\frac{1}{2}$ by $\frac{2}{3}$, by $\frac{3}{4}$, by $\frac{12}{16}$, by $\frac{18}{24}$.
7. Divide $\frac{3}{20}$ by 5, and multiply the quotient by 4.
8. Divide $6.25 by 2.5.
9. Add twelve and a half cents, ten dollars and ten cents, one hundred dollars, and one dollar and one half a cent.
10. From $120\frac{1}{3}$ take $75\frac{1}{4}$.

Ten Questions — Four Credits Each.

11. Multiply 1 year, 5 months, 6 days, 7 hours, and 8 minutes by 10.
12. How many square rods in 2 acres of land?
13. How many feet in 10 miles?
14. How many ounces in a ton of sugar?
15. How many cubic feet in a room 20 feet long, 18 feet wide, and 10 feet high?
16. Multiply 2.5 by .001, and divide the product by .05.

17. Add $\frac{1}{4}$ and the decimal fraction twenty-five hundredths.

18. Divide .001 by 50, and multiply the quotient by .2.

19. Divide $\frac{3}{4}$ of 24 by $\frac{2}{3}$.

20. Reduce £16, 17*s.* 5*d.* 1*far.*, to farthings.

Five Questions — Six Credits Each.

21. Write a promissory note, in which you promise to pay John Smith $1,000, one month after date, with interest at 1½ per cent. a month.

22. George Webster buys of John Smith, the grocer, the following articles: 1 sack of potatoes, 80 pounds, at 1½ cents a pound: 25 pounds of sugar, at 12½ cents a pound, and 6 dozen eggs, at 4 bits a dozen. Make out the grocer's bill.

23. Order Wm. C. Ralston to pay Peter Smith $25, and charge to you.

24. What is the interest of $400 for 2 years and 6 months, at 10 per cent. a year?

25. Multiply .2 by .2; subtract .004; divide the remainder by 9, and divide the quotient by .08.

S.

SET II.

TOTAL: SEVENTEEN QUESTIONS — FORTY CREDITS.

Ten Questions — Two Credits Each.

1. Five sixths plus three eighths plus seven twelfths minus three tenths.

2. Divide 8 by $\frac{3}{4}$, and explain the reason of the operation.

3. Multiply 24 by $\frac{5}{8}$, and explain the reason of the operation.

4. Multiply four ten-thousandths by six hundredths and divide the product by three tenths.

5. Divide $5 by ½ a cent.

6. From 1 rod take 2 inch.

7. How many square rods in 10 acres of land?

8. How much will 20 tons of wheat cost at 1½ cents a pound?

9. How many cubic inches in a box 12.6 feet long, 6.02 feet wide and, 2.4 feet high?

10. If ¾ of a piece of land cost $6,000, how much will ⅛ of it cost?

Five Questions—Four Credits Each.

11. You sell to John Doe, on the 1st of May, 1871, 20 pounds of sugar, at 15¾ cents a pound; 25 pounds of coffee, at 21½ cents a pound; 11 pounds of tea, at 87½ cents a pound. Make out the bill.

12. What is 13⅔ per cent. of 837 pounds of iron?

13. How many yards of cloth, ⅞ of a yard wide, will line 23⅓ yards that is 1¼ yards wide.

14. A drover bought 69 beeves at $28.75 a head, and sold 42 of them at $36.50 a head, and the rest at $37.75 a head; how much did he gain by the transaction?

15. An embankment 12 feet high and 4.5 feet thick contains 6,000 cubic feet; how long is it?

Two Questions—Five Credits Each.

16. Allowing that 4 persons can stand on 1 square rod of ground, how many persons can stand in a street 15 rods long and 35 feet wide?

17. 176,179 square inches are what units of higher denominations? S.

ARITHMETIC.

FOURTH GRADE.

SET I.

TOTAL: TWENTY-FIVE QUESTIONS — ONE HUNDRED CREDITS.

Ten Questions — Three Credits Each.

1. DIVIDE 153,598 by 29.
2. Add $\frac{4}{5}$, $\frac{3}{4}$, and $\frac{2}{3}$.
3. Multiply 96 by $\frac{7}{8}$, and divide the product by $\frac{2}{3}$.
4. Multiply $\frac{5}{8}$ by 4, and divide the product by 3.
5. Divide $1\frac{1}{2}$ by $1\frac{1}{3}$.
6. Multiply $10\frac{1}{2}$ by $2\frac{1}{2}$.
7. What cost $\frac{4}{5}$ yards of cloth, at $1.75 a yard?
8. Divide 625 by .25.
9. Multiply 10 by .01, and divide the product by 4.
10. Divide $100 by $12\frac{1}{2}$ cents.

Ten Questions — Four Credits Each.

11. What will 5 tons of sugar cost, at 10 cents a pound?

12. How many feet in 10 miles?

13. How many square feet on the floor of a room, 30 feet long, by 25 feet wide?

14. How many cubic feet in a box 6 feet long, 4 feet wide, and 3 feet high?

15. Write 1869 in Roman numerals.

16. Divide 125,425 by 1,000.

17. Add the following decimals: Seven tenths, twenty-five hundredths, and one hundred and five ten-thousandths.

18. Add $125\frac{1}{4}$, $75\frac{1}{8}$, $60\frac{1}{2}$.

19. If 7 oranges cost $\frac{3}{4}$ of a dollar, what part of a dollar will 5 oranges cost?

20. Reduce 15 degrees to seconds.

Five Questions — Six Credits Each.

21. What will 125 pounds of rice cost, at $1\frac{3}{4}$ cents a pound?

22. What is the interest on $125.50, for 3 months, at $1\frac{1}{2}$ per cent. per month?

23. John Smith hires of William Brown $100 payable in 3 months, at 2 per cent. a month, in U. S. gold coin. Write a promissory note, date it June 1, 1869, and sign John Smith's name.

24. What is the interest of $150 for 1 year and 6 months, at 10 per cent. a year?

25. Henry Dixon bought at the grocery store of Peter Brown, $12\frac{1}{2}$ pounds of sugar, at 10 cents a pound; $8\frac{1}{2}$ pounds of coffee, at 20 cents a pound, and 5 pounds of tea, at 75 cents a pound. Make out his bill and receipt it. S.

SET II.

PROBLEMS.

1. Paid $40.50 for a pile of wood: if I paid $33,75 a cord, how many cords were there?

2. Find the difference between 9 times $5.67, and 9 times $6.75.

3. If 29 pounds of butter cost $14.50, what cost 63 pounds?

4. Purchased 25 pieces of cloth, each containing 38 yards, at .$19\frac{1}{2}$ cents per yard; paid for it in flour at $7.41 per barrel; how many barrels did it take?

5. Reduce $\frac{24186}{190}$ to a mixed number.

6. Bought a cow and 254 sheep for $1,134$\frac{1}{2}$: the cow cost $55; what was the cost of one sheep?

7. From $3,259 take 12 eagles, 17 dimes.

8. What cost

9 yards silk at $1.10 per yard?
15 yards muslin at .13 per yard?
24 yards calico at .09 per yard?
6 yards gingham .45 per yard?
7 yards velvet at $6.75 per yard?

9. Add $\frac{39}{75}$, $\frac{29}{75}$, $\frac{9}{75}$, $\frac{38}{75}$, and reduce the answer to a mixed number.

10. A man having $8,127, spent $\frac{1}{27}$ of it; how much had he left?

MENTAL ARITHMETIC.

1. By selling 7 oranges for 55 cents, I lost 6 cents; what did the oranges cost apiece?

2. A man received $6 for 4 days' work; what should he receive for 12 days' work?

3. How many pounds, at 7 cents a pound, must be given for $6\frac{3}{8}$ yards, at 8 cents a yard?

4. How many men will it take to do as much work in 6 days as 3 men do in 10 days?

5. James earns $8 while John earns $12, how much has James earned when John has earned $60?

6. Bought $8\frac{2}{5}$ gallons of wine at $5 per gallon, and paid for it with flour at $8 per barrel; how many barrels did it take?

7. The sum of two numbers is 23; $\frac{1}{2}$ of them is 7, what is the other?

8. How many pears at 3 for 7 cents can you buy for 21 cents?

9. $\frac{1}{6}$ of my money is gold, $\frac{4}{6}$ bills, and the rest, which is $12, is silver; how much money have I?

10. How many fourths in 8? How many fourths in $\frac{2}{3}$ of 6?

SET III.

TOTAL: SEVENTEEN QUESTIONS — FIFTY CREDITS.

Ten Questions — Two Credits Each.

1. Divide 10,108,207 by 179.

2. Add two sevenths, three fifths, one third.

3. Multiply 21 by four sevenths, and explain the reason of the operation.

4. Divide 1.44 by .12, and multiply the quotient by the decimal three thousandths.

5. Divide $50 by 6¼ cents.

6. Multiply 2½ by 2½, and divide the product by 2.5.

7. How many square yards on the floor of a room 25.5 feet long and 20.5 feet wide?

8. A box containing 1,728 cubic inches is 12 inches wide, and 4 inches high: how long is it?

9. How many feet in 7 miles, 108 rods, 3 yards, 1 foot?

10. Reduce 1,001,100,100 cubic inches to higher denominations.

Five Questions — Four Credits Each.

11. From one hundred and one subtract one hundred one-millionths.

12. What is the product of six hundred twenty-five thousandths by forty-eight hundredths?

13. If the interest on $1 for one year is $.10, what is the interest on $25.50?

14. Into how many building lots, each containing .25 of an acre, can 5 acres be divided?

15. A house agent rents 7 tenements at $1.12½ a week, 5 at 1.25 a week, 11 at $1.50 a week: what do the rents amount to in a year?

Two Questions—Five Credits Each.

16. What will 3 miles of telegraph wire cost at 5 cents a foot?

17. A man bought a farm, containing 125 acres, for $2,562.50: for how much an acre must he sell to gain $1,250? S.

SET IV.

MENTAL ARITHMETIC.

1. If 9 men earn $72 in 8 days, how many dollars can they earn in 1 day?

2. 6 oranges were sold for 48 cents, and 12 cents were lost; what did each cost?

3. A man bought 18 yards of cloth at the rate of 2 yards for $9; what did the cloth cost him?

4. When apples were worth 2 cents apiece, and pears 3 cents apiece, 4 apples and 6 pears were given for oranges at 8 cents apiece; how many oranges did they buy?

5. If 3 men can do a piece of work in 6 days, how long will it take 4 men to do it?

6. If a man can cut 12 cords of wood in 3 days, how many cords can he cut in 9 days?

7. If you have corn enough to last 10 horses 1 month, how many horses would it last 2 months?

8. If a boy spend 20 cents for pears at 2 cents apiece, and sells them for 5 cents apiece, how much does he make on all?

9. A man can earn $8 while a boy can earn $5; how many dollars will both have earned when the man has earned $40?

10. If I buy peaches at rates of 2 for 6 cents, and sell 4 for 24 cents, how much do I gain on each?

PROBLEMS.

1. What cost:

    920 bushels wheat, at $3.05 a bushel?
    720 bushels corn, at $0.875 a bushel?
    900 bushels meal, at $2.09?

2. Multiply 76,009 by 29, and divide the product by 97.

3. From nine hundred and ten thousand and two, take six hundred and nine thousand and four.

4. Multiply $6,080.009 by 92.

5. Take $0.09 from the sum of $892, $685, $701, $9,865, $74,900, and $8,962.

6. Reduce $\frac{67231}{13}$ to a mixed number.

7. A farm cost $7,090.05, a boat $96,000, and a ship 4 times as much as both; what did they altogether cost?

8. How many five cent pieces in $720.90?

9. Multiply 9,080 by 8,009.

10. Divide 624,921 by 98.

SET V.

MENTAL ARITHMETIC.

1. I paid 40 cents for 8 marbles, and sold them so as to gain 8 cents; what did I get for each marble?

2. If 12 men can do a piece of work in 4 days, how many men will it take to do it in one day?

3. If 3 apples cost 18 cents, what will 2 cost?

4. If you take 7 times 9 from 8 times 8, what will remain?

5. If a lemon cost 6 cents and a melon 11 cents, what will 1 lemon and 4 melons cost?

6. Two boys commenced playing marbles; each had 14 when they began; when they quit one had 17; how many had the other?

7. 97 — 7 — 7 — 7 — 9 — 9 — 9 — 8 — 8 — 6 — 6 — 6 — 7 = ?

8. 54 + 7 + 7 + 9 + 9 + 7 + 8 + 8 + 7 + 9 + 7 + 5 + 6 = ?

9. 78 — 4 + 8 — 9 + 6 — 5 + 8 — 7 + 3 — 4 + 8 — 6 = ?

10. If a man can do a piece of work in 12 days, how long will it take 3 men to do it?

PROBLEMS.

1. Multiply 729 by 87.
2. Take 22,007 from 45,006.
3. Add 280, 396, 984, 596, 898, 724, and subtract 2,506 from the sum.
4. Reduce $12\frac{5}{7}$ to an improper fraction.
5. A horse cost $250, a farm 309 times as much; what would horse and farm cost?
6. Divide the sum of 869, 9,864, 30,862 by 9.
7. Add 7,646, 98,684, 386, 85, 9, 88,964.
8. Paid $92,085 for a farm, $\frac{1}{5}$ as much for a house; what did both cost?
9. What cost 616 head of cattle at $37 each?
10. At $8 per pair, how many pairs boots could $29,008 purchase?

ARITHMETIC.

FIFTH GRADE.

SET I.

TWENTY-FIVE QUESTIONS — FOUR CREDITS EACH.

1. WHAT is the sum of 405 + 697 + 842 + 587 + 488 + 598?

2. What is the sum of one million and four hundred thousand, plus two hundred and ten thousand, plus seventy-five thousand and forty?

3. Write 125 in Roman numerals.

4. Multiply 4,456 by 204.

5. Divide 153,598 by 29.

6. Multiply 45,000 by 2,000.

7. Divide 125,000 by 8.

8. Divide 124,525 by 1,000.

9. Multiply 125 by 4, and divide the product by 8.

10. Divide 144,125 by 12,000.

11. Add the decimals four and twenty-five hundredths; two and four hundredths; five tenths; one and two hundredths; seventy-five and seventy-five hundredths.

12. From eight and twenty-five hundredths, take four and thirty-nine hundredths.

13. From one and five hundredths, take twenty-five hundredths.

14. Multiply four and twenty-five hundredths by five.

15. Multiply one and two hundredths by ten.

16. What is the sum of four dollars and twenty-five cents, plus five cents, plus one hundred dollars and ten cents, plus ten dollars and twelve and a half cents?

17. Multiply four dollars and twenty-five cents by nine.

18 Write twenty-four ninety-fifths as a fraction.

19. In $20\frac{4}{5}$, how many fifths?

20. Change $\frac{43}{4}$ to a mixed number.

21. Reduce $\frac{24}{48}$ to its lowest terms.

22. What is $\frac{2}{3}$ of 9? Write out the operation in words.

23. How many pounds of butter, worth 25 cents a pound, can be bought for 400 pounds of cheese, worth 10 cents a pound?

24. If 8 horses cost $1,200, how much will 40 horses cost?

25. From 1,000 substract 125, multiply the remainder by 4, and divide the product by 20.

SET II.

TOTAL: SEVENTEEN QUESTIONS — FIFTY CREDITS.

Ten Questions — Two Credits Each.

1. Add 47 to 98. Why do you carry the left hand figure after adding 8 and 7?

2. Subtract 59 from 86 and explain the reason of the operation.

3. Divide 842 by 3 and explain why you suppose the remainder of each separate figure to be placed *before* the next succeeding figure.

4. From ten thousand and eighty-two take one thousand and nine.

5. $47 + 35 + 97 + 85 + 92 \times 7 + 109 =$ how many?

6. Multiply 1,057 by 309.

7. Multiply 25 by 48, and tell what denomination is obtained in multiplying 2 by 8.

8. Divide 378,000 by 12,000.

9. Divide one by two.

10. Divide 7,831 by 15.

Five Questions—Four Credits Each.

11. Multiply 45,125 by 2,500.

12. From one and two tenths subtract five thousandths.

13. 56 knives cost $336, how much will 57 knives cost?

14. How many pounds of sugar, at 15 cents a pound, will a man receive in exchange for 1,000 pounds of wheat, at 2 cents a pound?

15. How much will a baker receive for 48 pounds of crackers, at 14 cents a pound, and 128 loaves of bread, at 9 cents a loaf?

Two Questions—Five Credits Each.

16. If 33 pickets are used in building one rod of fence, how many pickets will be used in building a fence around a lot 16 rods long and 15 rods wide?

17. How many times can 114 be subtracted from 2,622?

SET III.

PROBLEMS.

1. From thirty thousand and twenty, take twenty-nine thousand and twenty-nine.

2. Multiply 40,706 by 90,700.

3. Reduce $19\frac{25}{75}$ to an improper fraction.

4. It is 25,000 miles around the earth: after traveling 9,374 miles how many miles of the journey remain?

5. What is the cost of 28 barrels of sugar, each containing 196 pounds, at 14 cents per pound?

6. Write in words 71,036.

7. Divide seven hundred and five thousand one hundred and eighty-four by eight.

8. A man bought 2 houses: he paid $2,500 for one of them, and $1,000 for the other; what did he gain by selling both for $4,326?

9. At $7 each, how many hats can I purchase for $12,426?

10. Bought 97 horses at $147 each, and 136 cows at $72 each; what was the cost of all?

MENTAL ARITHMETIC.

1. By selling 5 peaches for 30 cents, 5 cents were lost, what was the cost of one peach?

2. How many tops, at 9 cents each, can you buy for the sum of 72 cents and 9 cents?

3. Bought 9 balls for 72 cents, and sold four of them for 36 cents, did I gain or lose, and how much?

4. The sum of two numbers is 27; if 19 is the larger, what is three times the smaller?

5. In $8\frac{7}{9}$ how many ninths?

6. 7 times 6 are how many times 8?

7. 4 pears at 3 cents each, and 3 peaches at 5 cents each, were given for 9 figs; what was the cost of each fig?

8. 12 cents is $\frac{1}{3}$ of my money, how many lemons at 4 cents each can I buy for all my money?

9. 4 times 6 cents was 8 times the price of an apple; what were 5 apples worth.

10. $12 \times 2 \div 3 \times 2 \div 4 \div 2 + 8 + 9 + 5 \div 3 = ?$

ARITHMETIC.

SIXTH GRADE.

SET I.

1. Add the following five numbers: Twenty thousand two hundred. Four hundred sixteen thousand fifty-four. Nine thousand seven hundred eighty-nine. Forty-eight thousand six hundred twelve. One hundred one thousand nine hundred nine.

2. Add the following six numbers: 205,818; 31,719; 84,600; 207; 199,991; 95.

3. Subtract three hundred seventy-six thousand seventy-two, from eight hundred twenty-three thousand three hundred two.

4. Multiply 87,093 by 9.

5. Multiply 6,435 by 74.

6. Divide 660,827 by 8.

7. From 37,216, subtract 9,109, and multiply the result by 12.

8. $3{,}824 + 219 + 1{,}008 - 875 \div 5 = ?$

SET II.

MENTAL ARITHMETIC AND COMBINATIONS.

1. If $\frac{1}{5}$ of a pound of crackers is worth 3 cents, how much is a pound worth?

2. How many eggs in $\frac{3}{4}$ of a dozen?

3. How many days are there in 3 weeks and 3 days?

4. How many dimes are there in half a dollar?

5. If cream is worth 20 cents a quart, how much must I give for a pint?

6. How much must be added to three 10's to make five 9's?

7. If a boy is 3 feet 4 inches high, how many inches high is he?

8. Six 7's, less 2, are how many 5's?

9. How many ounces in 3 pounds?

10. If 3 oranges cost 15 cents, what will 2 oranges cost?

11. $11 \times 11 - 1 \div 10 \times 4 - 6 \div 7 \div 4 \times 5 = ?$

12. $12 \times 11 - 2 - 15 - 15 \div 10 \times 6 - 10 = ?$

13. $13 + 15 \div 4 \times 9 + 1 \div 8 \times 12 + 4 = ?$

14. $14 + 16 + 30 \div 5 \times 3 - 1 \div 7 \times 5 = ?$

15. $15 \div 5 \times 3 \times 3 + 13 - 15 - 10 = ?$

16. $16 + 16 \div 4 \times 12 + 3 \div 11 \times 5 + 5 = ?$

17. $17 + 3 \times 2 + 2 \div 6 \times 10 + 30 - 0 = ?$

18. $18 \div 9 - 2 + 24 \div 4 \times 9 + 0 - 4 = ?$

19. $9 + 11 \div 3 \times 7 + 2 \div 6 \times 12 + 6 = ?$

20. $20 - 6 \div 7 \times 2 \times 2 \times 2 + 8 \div 6 \times 5 = ?$

GEOGRAPHY.

FIRST GRADE.

SET I.

FIFTEEN QUESTIONS — FIVE CREDITS EACH.

1. Largest five cities in the United States?
2. Largest five rivers?
3. Largest three rivers in New England?
4. Extent and area of the United States?
5. The great physical regions of the United States?
6. Where are the desert regions of the United States?
7. Products of Texas?
8. Climate of Great Britain? Why?
9. What countries are included in the warm zone of Europe?
10. What are the products of this part of Europe?
11. For what is Asia noted?
12. Population of China?
13. What is the length in miles of a degree of longitude on the Equator?
14. What is the horizon?
15. Highest mountain peak in the United States?

SET II.

TOTAL: FIFTEEN QUESTIONS — ONE HUNDRED CREDITS.

Ten Questions — Five Credits Each.

1. NAME and locate six large cities in South America.

2. Four leading exports of California?

3. What are the great natural divisions of the United States?

4. State the peculiar characteristics of the climate of the different sections of the United States.

5. Mention the two leading States in each of the the following particulars: (1) size; (2) population; (3) manufactures; (4) coal; (5) gold; (6) wheat.

6. Name and locate the largest six cities of the United States, and state in round numbers the population of each of the largest three.

7. What are the most striking physical features of South America?

8. Name the four principal cities of the island of Great Britain, and state for what each is distinguished.

9. Physical characteristics and peculiar animals of Africa.

10. Name and locate the four principal cities of France, and name the four principal rivers.

Five Questions — Ten Credits Each.

11. Name the principal plateau and the largest plain of Asia? of North America?

12. Climate, vegetation, and peculiar animals of Australia?

13. How does China compare, in size and population, with the United States?

14. Name and locate ten of the principal commercial cities of the world — no two in any one country.

15. Name two countries distinguished for each of the following particulars: (1) coffee; (2) silk; (3) opium; (4) cotton; (5) indigo; (6) caoutchouc.

S.

SET II.

TWENTY QUESTIONS — FIVE CREDITS EACH.

1. What two motions has the earth? Which of these causes the change of seasons?

2. What is a water-shed?

3. Mention three uses of rivers.

4. In what situations do commercial cities grow up? and in what, manufacturing cities?

5. How does South America compare in vegetation with any other continent? Why is this?

6. What are the exports of Rio Janeiro? of Buenos Ayres?

7. What are the pampas of South America?

8. Name the mountain ranges of Europe.

9. Describe the surface and productions of the southeastern part of Europe.

10. What three groups of islands near the coast of Scotland?

11. Through what water would a vessel pass in sailing from Stockholm to Venice?

12. What countries of Europe are called the five great powers?

13. Describe five of the chief rivers of Europe.

14. Describe the climate and vegetation of Australia.

15. What countries of Europe produce silk, olives, and wine?

16. Name ten rivers of the United States that flow into the Atlantic.

17. Name six large cities situated on the Mississippi River and its branches.

18. Name all the mountain ranges of the Appalachian system.

19. What countries of Africa border on the Mediterranean Sea?

20. Bound Alaska, and name its rivers, islands, and products.

SET III.

1. In what directions, on what waters, and with what cargo would a vessel sail from San Francisco to New York?

2. Name the leading commercial cities, situated on the Atlantic, in the western hemisphere.

3. Bound the State of Pennsylvania.

4. Through what States and Territories does the Pacific Railroad pass?

5. State the situation of the following cities: London; St. Petersburg; Paris; Yeddo; Calcutta.

6. In what directions, on what waters, would a steamer sail from Bombay to Liverpool, taking the most direct route?

7. What is the width of the Torrid Zone in geographical miles?

8. Suppose a place has no latitude or longitude, where would it be located?

9. What constitutes the British Empire?

10. Name the principal cotton-growing regions of the world. S.

GEOGRAPHY.

SECOND GRADE.

SET I.

TOTAL: FIFTEEN QUESTIONS — ONE HUNDRED CREDITS.

Ten Questions — Five Credits Each.

1. MOUNTAIN ranges, three principal cities and population of North America.

2. (*a*) Name four principal mountain ranges; (*b*) four principal rivers; (*c*) four principal cities; (*d*) four principal bays, of the United States.

3. What are the characteristics of that part of the United States lying between the Rocky Mountains and the Sierra Nevada?

4. Why is the Great Salt Lake in Utah filled with salt water instead of fresh?

5. Name two States that excel in each of the following products: (*a*) cotton; (*b*) tobacco; (*c*) coal; (*d*) Indian corn.

6. What natural division of the United States is the most fertile?

7. Name the four principal seaports of the United States.

8. What are the vegetable products and exports of South America?

9. Why has Africa fewer rivers than South America?

10. (*a*) Name two mountain ranges, (*b*) four prin-

cipal rivers, and (*c*) four principal cities of Asia. (*d*) Four principal seas.

Five Questions — Ten Credits Each.

11. What articles are exported from India?

12. (*a*) What countries produce tea? (*b*) coffee? (*c*) cotton? (*d*) sugar.

13. (*a*) Where is Melbourne? (*b*) Honolulu? (*c*) Yokohama? (*d*) Calcutta?

14. (*a*) Name the four principal cities, (*b*) four principal rivers, (*c*) four principal straits, (*d*) four principal seas of Europe.

15. (*a*) Where is the Yukon river? (*b*) Humboldt river (*c*) San Diego? (*d*) Sitka? S.

SET II.

TWELVE QUESTIONS — SIX CREDITS EACH.

1. Name three capes and three islands on the Pacific coast of North America.

2. Of what islands are the West Indies composed?

3. Give the extent of the Pacific highlands.

4. Name five great rivers that flow into the Pacific Ocean.

5. What is the highest portion of the Andes?

6. Name three cities having an elevated situation in the Andes mountains.

7. Why is South America more moist as a whole than other continents?

8. Name the four principal capes of Africa.

9. Name three rivers that flow into the Indian Ocean.

10. Describe the climate of the northern part of Australia.

11. Where is the Crimea?

12. Where is the Baltic Sea?

SET III.

FIFTEEN QUESTIONS—FIVE CREDITS EACH.

1. Define a Mediterranean Sea; an inland sea.

2. Name three principal indentations on the eastern coast of North America.

3. Why are there no large rivers in South America flowing into the Pacific?

4. Why does the valley of the Amazon support so luxuriant a growth of vegetation?

5. Describe the Pacific highlands.

6. What determines the course of a river?

7. Locate San Francisco and Havana.

8. Describe the Colorado river.

9. Which is the largest manufacturing city in the United States?

10. Why does the interior of Mexico contain the largest part of the population?

11. What river systems belong wholly to the United States?

12. Why is South America, as a whole, more moist than any other continent?

13. Name three States that rank high in manufactures.

14. Name five principal articles exported by the United States.

15. What are the most northern, eastern, and western points of South America?

SET IV.

TEN QUESTIONS—FIVE CREDITS EACH.

1. Bound South America.

2. Name the countries of South America that lie wholly north of the Equator. Those crossed by the Equator.

3. What are the political divisions of Western Europe?

4. What parts of Europe are valued mainly for iron and copper mines?

5. Bound the country of which Dublin is the capital.

6. Draw a map of the part of South America that has no capital.

7. Name the five principal cities in the country of Europe which rank first in commercial importance.

8. Name four large rivers of South America in order of their size.

9. What parts of South America are valued principally for grazing?

10. What cities of South America are situated upon a mountain chain?

GEOGRAPHY.

THIRD GRADE.

SET I.

TEN QUESTIONS — TEN CREDITS EACH.

1. WHAT river between the United States and Mexico? between Oregon and Washington Territory?

2. Name the States that border on the Gulf of Mexico.

3. Name three branches of the Mississippi River; two of the Ohio.

4. Name the capitals of Louisiana, North Carolina, Tennessee, Ohio.

5. Name five rivers of the United States that empty into the Atlantic Ocean. Three that flow into the Gulf of Mexico.

6. What States have "plains" and "prairies?"

7. Name five countries of South America, with their capitals.

8. Name two rivers that flow into the Caspian Sea.

9. What mountains between Spain and France? between Italy and Switzerland? between Europe and Asia?

10. In what zone is the United States? Cuba? Borneo?

GEOGRAPHY.

FOURTH GRADE.

SET I.

TWENTY QUESTIONS — FIVE CREDITS EACH.

1. NAME the oceans.
2. What is a republic?
3. Name the largest river, lake, sea, and city in the world.
4. Largest gulf and bay in North America.
5. What Europeans made discoveries and settlements in North America?
6. What can you say about Cortez?
7. How many States in the United States, and which is the largest?
8. Name four great rivers in the United States.
9. The two largest cities in the United States?
10. How long did the War of the Revolution last, and when was the Declaration of Independence made?
11. Where is the Mississippi Valley?
12. Principal agricultural products of the United States.
13. What is the largest city in the Southern States?
14. Where is Chicago?
15. Name a State noted for each of the following

products: (1) gold; (2) cotton; (3) sugar; (4) silver.

16. Name and locate the largest city in the United States.

17. Largest city, river, and bay in California?

18. Name the Pacific States.

19. What is the highest mountain peak in Asia?

20. Name the largest four cities in the world.

SET II.

TWENTY-FIVE QUESTIONS — TWO CREDITS EACH.

1. Where are Buenos Ayres and Rio Janeiro?

2. Name two mountain ranges of South America.

3. Bound Massachusetts.

4. Give the capital cities of the New England States.

5. Name two capes on the western coast of North America.

6. Name two rivers flowing into the Arctic Ocean.

7. Name the largest three of the West India Islands.

8. Name two capes of South America.

9. Describe the Danube River.

10. Name the capital cities of England, Austria, Sweden, Spain, and Russia.

11. Bound France.

12. Where are Philadelphia and Dublin?

13. Describe Amoor River.

14. Mention five seas which are in and around Asia.

15. Mention the largest three cities in the United States.

GEOGRAPHY.

FIFTH GRADE.

SET I.

TEN QUESTIONS — FIVE CREDITS EACH.

1. Define peninsula, isthmus, strait.

2. What is meant by latitude? longitude?

3. In what direction does the Rocky Mountain system extend, and through what four countries does it extend?

4. What States raise cotton? tobacco? cattle?

5. Name ten States that touch the Mississippi River.

6. Name the capitals of the States mentioned in your last answer.

7. Name three rivers of the Atlantic slope that form boundary lines between States, and name the States separated by each.

8. Name five lakes through which a ship would pass in floating from Chicago to the ocean.

9. Name the largest State; the smallest; the one most thickly inhabited; one that is a peninsula; one that borders on the Pacific Ocean.

10. Name ten Territories.

SET II.

FIFTEEN QUESTIONS — FIVE CREDITS EACH.

1. What are the natural divisions of land?

2. What is the largest city on the western continent?

3. Principal river and mountain range in North America? in South America?

4. What great mountain ranges in Asia?

5. Who discovered North America, and when?

6. What wild animals are found in North America?

7. In what does Pennsylvania excel every State in the Union? California?

8. What are raised in the Western States?

9. What States produce cotton and sugar?

10. Name three great rivers of South America? two capes?

11. Largest country and largest city of South America?

12. Principal productions of South America?

13. Largest city of France? Prussia? Russia? Austria?

14. What is the most populous empire in the world, and what is its capital?

15. What two great rivers in Asia?

SPELLING.

FIRST GRADE.

SET I.

TOTAL: ONE HUNDRED CREDITS.

Twenty-five Words — Two Credits Each.

1. Retrievable.
2. Receevable.
3. Unexpresable.
4. Unlimitly.
5. Masheen.
6. Sfericle.
7. Reccomendashun.
8. Clenlyness.
9. Pernishious.
10. Desicive.
11. Exibet.
12. Numness.
13. Cirkuit.
14. Calliko.
15. Acquited.
16. Monkies.
17. Centinels.
18. Sheeves.
19. Alegatur.
20. Liveing.
21. Disagreeable.
22. Flys.
23. Ocazionally.
24. Parigraf.
25. Cillindricall.

Twenty-five credits.

[One credit off for each word misspelled, one off for each misplaced capital, and one for any important error in punctuation.]

Copy and correct the spelling, punctuation, and capitals of the following extract from Walter Scott. The spelling of the proper names is correct as printed.

" have you confesed yourself Brother said the Templar Guilbert and have you heard mass this morning that you may perrill your life so frankly. i am fiter to meet death than thou art answered the Disinherited Knight for by this name the stranger had recorded himself in the book of the tourney. then take your place in the lists said de bois guilbert and take your last look upon the Sun for this night thou shalt sleep in paradise. grant mercy for thy courtesy replied the Disinhereted Knight and to requite it I advise the to take a fresh horse and a new lance for by my honor you will need both."

GEOGRAPHICAL NAMES.

Ten Credits.

1. Tenese.
2. Indianna.
3. Connetticut.
4. Cincinnatti.
5. Masachusets.
6. Venezwala.
7. Himmalah Mountains.
8. Reeo Janaro.
9. Bordo.
10. San deeago.

Fifteen Credits.

[One credit off for each misspelled word and each misplaced capital.]

" Orthography treats of letters, sylabels, seperate words and speling."

" the first word of every distinct Sentence should begin with a Capital.

" the orthography of our language is atendid with much unsertinty and perplecksity."

" Words of one sylable, and words accented on the last sylable ending with a single consonent, preseded by a single vowell doubble the final consonent on reseiving an additional terminashun beginning with a vowell: as rob, robbing; acquit, acquiting." S.

SET II.

TOTAL: FIFTY CREDITS.

Ten Words — One Credit Each.

1. Retreiveable.
2. Receivable.
3. Terrific.
4. Carnivurous.

5. Inexpressable.
6. Fullfillment.
7. Resussitate.
8. Tipograficle.
9. Maintainence.
10. Intamitly.

Twenty Credits.

[One credit off for each word misspelled, each capital omitted or misplaced, and each error in punctuation.]

"There are also subterranian pasages often more than a foot in Diameter and perfectly sillindrecal which extend downward three or four feet and then branch out horry-zontaly on every side sometimes to the distance of sevral hundred feet before sutch struktures the piramids of egypt and the acquiducts of rome would lose all their selebrety and dwindel into insigniffecanse."

Ten Credits.

[One credit off for each word wrongly spelled.]

"The oposition to the revveneu meazures indused the British Parliament to revoak all dutys layed in 1767, except that of three pense per pound on tea; but as the peepel were contending against the prinsipal of 'taxashun without representasion,' and not agenst the amount of taxes imposed, the consession was not satisfactory."

Ten Credits.

[One credit off for each misspelled word and each misplaced capital.]

"The Andez mountain region, with the planes laying at its eastern foot, is divided into six countrys: the united states of columbia and ecquidore, lyeing north of the amazon; peroo and bolivvia; chele and the argeentean republic, laying south of the ammazon." S.

WORD ANALYSIS.

SET I.

TWENTY-FIVE QUESTIONS — FOUR CREDITS EACH.

1. DEFINE *abs* and *bene*.
2. Write words containing *e* and *retro*.
3. Define the words just written.
4. Define *introversion* and *preterit*.
5. Define *apogee* and *chirography*.
6. Define *dys* and *entomo*.
7. Write words containing *helio* and *litho*.
8. Define these words.
9. Define *osteology* and *philology*.
10. Write words containing *syl* and *peri*.
11. Define the words just written.
12. Write two words containing Saxon prefixes.
13. Write two words having the prefix *anti*.
14. Define *omnipotent* and *equilateral*.
15. Define the suffixes *ment* and *ferous*.
16. Write words containing the suffixes *ose* and *ism*.
17. Define *mandatory* and *asteroid*.
18. Define the suffixes in *drunkard* and *vesicle*.
19. Give some rule concerning the omission of final *e*.

26\. Give two examples in which *ie* final is changed into *y*.

21. Form two derivatives from *unite* by the use of prefixes.

22. Form two derivatives from *method* by the use of suffixes.

23. Define the suffixes in *learned* and *alarming*.

24. Mention two or more suffixes characteristic of verbs.

25. Mention two or more suffixes characteristic of adjectives.

SET II.

FIFTEEN QUESTIONS — FOUR CREDITS EACH.

Name and define each prefix, root, and suffix, and give a full definition of the whole word.

1. Incorporate.	8. Exhibit.
2. Colloquial.	9. Accident.
3. Supervision.	10. Anticipate.
4. Detract.	11. Homicide.
5. Retrograde.	12. Construct.
6. Attentive.	13. Dejection.
7. Subscribe.	14. Supercilious.

15. Metropolis.

S.

SPELLING.

SECOND GRADE.

SET I.

TOTAL: FIFTY CREDITS.

Twenty Words — One Credit Each.

1. Shandeleer.
2. Mashene.
3. Relief.
4. Sferical.
5. Retreeve.
6. Fasecious.
7. Tecknicle.
8. Reccomend.
9. Clenlynes.
10. Acheeve.
11. Pernishus.
12. Synonym.
13. Tirranize.
14. Tommyhock.
15. Musilage.
16. Desicive.
17. Cristalize.
18. Exibit.
19. Morallize.
20. Solemly.

Thirty Credits.

[One credit off for each misspelled word.]

Correct the spelling and the capital letters of the following paragraph: —

"Portions of our Country have occasionaly been overun with swarmes of miscaled Grasshopers, which are only species of Locusts, but little less distructive than the Migratory locusts of the east. The name *locust* which is derived from the latin, and means 'a burnt place,' is highly expresive of the desolation caused by these insects. So well do the arabians know and feel there power, that one of their poets represents a locust saying to mohammed:

'We are the army of the great god.' Numerous reptiles such as snaiks, turkles, lizzards, frogs, and todes, also feed upon them." S.

SET II.

TWO CREDITS EACH.

1. Advantageous.
2. Separation.
3. Courtesy.
4. Caterpillar.
5. Fitted.
6. Succulent.
7. Mucilage.
8. Fusible.
9. Crucible.
10. Logarithms.
11. Proselyte.
12. Emaciate.
13. Cognizance.
14. Complaisance.
15. Bronchia.
16. Exhilarate.
17. Bubble.
18. Pierce.
19. Hypocrite.
20. Pleurisy.
21. Porridge.
22. Scythe.
23. Traffic.
24. Marchioness.
25. Tranquility.
26. Precipice.
27. Bacchanal.
28. Gauge.
29. Gnarl.
30. Choleric.
31. Tyrannize.
32. Hosiery.
33. Initiate.
34. Acquiring.
35. Synchronism.
36. Synonym.
37. Synthesis.
38. Michaelmas.
39. Contagious.
40. Judgment.
41. Elision.
42. Pavilion.
43. Strychnine.
44. Bulletin.
45. Movably.
46. Abolish.
47. Diligent.
48. Quiescence.
49. Liturgy.
50. Fallible.

SPELLING.

THIRD GRADE.

SET I.

TOTAL: ONE HUNDRED CREDITS.

Fifteen Words — Three Credits Each.

[One credit for correct spelling in each sentence, and one check for each misspelled word; two credits for each correct sentence.]

USE each word or phrase in a complete sentence, which shall show that you understand the meaning.

1. Intrinsic value.
2. Precepts of religion.
3. Vague idea.
4. Draught of water.
5. Seizure of the thief.
6. Model of the machine.
7. Squirrel.
8. Breadth.
9. Scythe.
10. Avidity.
11. Antipathy.
12. Residence.
13. Their anxiety.
14. Bruise.
15. Funeral hearse.

Ten Words — Two Credits Each.

[One credit for spelling, and one for the sentence and definition.]

1. Precise.
2. External.
3. Parallel.
4. Tenacious.
5. Equivalent..
6. Brilliant.
7. Acute.
8. Vivid.
9. Inadequate.
10. Solitary.

Five Questions — Two Credits Each.

1. What is a sentence?
2. Write a word containing an apostrophe.

3. Show the use of a caret in a word or sentence.
4. Write a word to show the use of the diæresis.
5. Show the use of quotation marks.

Three Questions — Five Credits Each.

6. Give five cases in which capital letters ought to be used. (One credit for each case.)
7. Write the rule for dropping the final *e*.
8. Give the rule for forming the plural of nouns.

Ten Abbreviations — One Credit Each.

1. A. M.	6. Do.
2. Cr.	7. 8vo.
3. A. D.	8. Sen.
4. Cwt.	9. M. C.
5. e. g.	10. M. D.

S.

SET II.

[One credit for correct spelling, and one for the correct use of each word in a sentence.]

1. Aukward.	6. Callico.
2. Gauge.	7. Handkerchief.
3. Repreive.	8. Acquited.
4. Sirkit.	9. Saleable.
5. Outragious.	10. Merryer.

Twenty Credits.

[One credit off for each misspelled word and each misplaced capital.]

Correct the spelling, punctuation, and capitals :—

"Amung the monkies of the old world their is a grate variety in shaip and size. the Monkies near the cape of good hope offen desend from the Mountains into the planes to pilage gardens and When they are on these expedishuns they plase centinells to guard agenst Surprize. the american monkies wich are found in grate numbers in the forrests of south america difer very much from those of asia and africa whitch we have allready discribed." S.

SET III.

1. Guerdon.
2. Seizure.
3. Courtesy.
4. Bubble.
5. Strychnine.
6. Sleazy.
7. Feign.
8. Gouge.
9. Neigh.
10. Gnarl.
11. Qualm.
12. Siege.
13. Wierd.
14. Judgment.
15. Discipline.
16. Business.
17. Chintz.
18. Yacht.
19. Tranquility.
20. Precedes.
21. Drought.
22. Pageantry.
23. Saccharine.
24. Rheumatic.
25. Lachrymose.
26. Raspberry.
27. Rhapsody.
28. Seraglio.
29. Tranquilize.
30. Paroxysm.
31. Bacchanal.
32. Analyze.
33. Machinate.
34. Pleurisy.
35. Archetype.
36. Marchioness.
37. Architect.
38. Paradigm.
39. Loving.
40. Complacence.
41. Hypocrite.
42. Receive.
43. Ghost.
44. Scythe.
45. Circuit.
46. Traffic.
47. Sheathe.
48. Tierce.
49. Skim.
50. Foreman.

SPELLING.

FOURTH GRADE.

SET I.

[One credit for the correct spelling of each word, and one for its correct use in a sentence.]

1. Beleef.
2. Babboon.
3. Forhead.
4. Programme.
5. Phrigid.
6. Curable.
7. Differing.
8. Malishus.
9. Conceit.
10. Phisycian.

Thirty Credits.

[One credit off for each misspelled word and each misplaced capital.]

Correct the spelling, punctuation and capitals :—

"the knawing quadrupeds whitch are so named on account of the peculiar Character of there front teath, or incizers are formed for feeding upon the harder kinds of vegitable mater such as nutts and grane and the rutes and twigs of Trees this divizion of animals, includes the Squirels beevers, Marmots porkupines Rats and Mice the Cavies or guinea pigs of south america and the Rabits and hairs."

S.

SET II.

ONE HUNDRED CREDITS.

Twenty Words — Four Credits Each.

[One credit for correct spelling in each sentence, and one check for each word in the sentence misspelled; three credits for the correct use of words or phrases.]

Use the words and phrases to form a complete sentence, which shall show that you understand the meaning of the words given.

1. Slothful habits.
2. Ready answer.
3. Noxious insects.
4. Enormous waste.
5. Genteel manners.
6. Salubrious climate.
7. Illustrious character.
8. Contagious plague.
9. Fierce quarrel.
10. Atrocious murder.
11. Receipt.
12. Conceive.
13. Condemn.
14. Deceitful.
15. Morose.
16. Conquer.
17. Celestial.
18. Cocoon.
19. Vineyard.
20. Courageous.

Ten Abbreviations — Two Credits Each.

1. A. M.
2. A. D.
3. D. C.
4. i. e
5. inst.
6. P. S.
7. 4to.
8. e. g
9. LL. D.
10 ult.

S.

SPELLING.

FIFTH GRADE.

SET I.

[One credit for the correct spelling of each word, and one credit for its correct use in a sentence.]

1. Deafnes.
2. Mufin.
3. Alchohol.
4. Shaveing.
5. Theives.
6. Elefant.
7. Aligatur.
8. Musquito.
9. Sypress.
10. Liveing.

Thirty Credits.

[One credit off for each word wrongly spelled, and each misplaced capital.]

"how meny catterpillers there are this summer said willie brown what dissagreable uggley things they are to — they were not hear last month but now they are all over the trees and on the ground as thick as flys where did they all come from !

"willie was so delited with his buterfly that he ran and called uncle john and aunt mary to come to sea it, uncle john told willie that this kind of buterfly was named berenice after a queen of syria who was selebrated for her buty." S.

SET II.

ONE HUNDRED CREDITS.

Twenty-five Words — Three Credits Each.

Use each word and phrase in constructing a sentence, which shall show that you understand the meaning.

Two credits for spelling, and one check for each word misspelled in the sentence.

One credit for each correct sentence.

1. Spicy nutmeg.
2. Juicy melon.
3. Thievish magpie.
4. Yellow canary bird.
5. Scaring turkeys.
6. Chloroform.
7. Laudanum.
8. Biscuit.
9. Raisin.
10. Omelet.
11. Gingham apron.
12. Dingy collar.
13. Cupboard.
14. Depot.
15. A steel scythe.
16. A gauze sieve.
17. Acquire property.
18. Scrub the porch.
19. Height of the ridge
20. Piece of thread.
21. Tough steak.
22. Square field.
23. Genteel mamma.
24. Avenge the affront.
25. Yawning chasm.

Fifteen Abbreviations — One Credit Each.

1. A. M.
2. A. D.
3. Att'y.
4. Bbl.
5. Co.
6. Cr.
7. Cts.
8. Dr.
9. Etc.
10. Geo.
11. Jr.
12. Lbs.
13. Oz.
14. 4to.
15. U. S.

Ten Words from Oral Instruction — One Credit Each.

1. Lilac.
2. Vermilion.
3. Granite.
4. Chimpanzee.
5. Giraffe.
6. Llama.
7. Rhubarb.
8. Cocoa.
9. Coffee.
10. Vanilla.

S.

UNITED STATES HISTORY.

FIRST GRADE.

SET I.

TEN QUESTIONS — TEN CREDITS EACH.

1. WHEN, and by whom, was Virginia settled? Massachusetts? New York? Pennsylvania?

2. What were the principal wars of the Colonies up to the time of the American Revolution?

3. What connection had George Washington with Colonial history?

4. What causes led to the Declaration of Independence?

5. Who was James Otis? Patrick Henry? Samuel Adams?

6. Who was king of England during the American Revolution? who were his prime ministers?

7. What difficulties did Washington encounter as commander-in-chief of the American army?

8. Give an account of the sufferings and patriotism of the army at Valley Forge.

9. What aid did France extend to the United States in the War of the Revolution?

10. Name the principal battles of the war of secession? S.

SET II.

TEN QUESTIONS—TEN CREDITS EACH.

1. What civilized people first settled the territory of New Mexico?

2. What was the object of the French in their Mississippi explorations?

3. When did the Dutch authority in New York end?

4. With whom did the Indians usually side in the contests between the English and French Colonists? Why?

5. When did the domination of the French in the northern part of the continent cease?

6. What nation contributed largely to the success of the Americans in their struggle for Independence?

7. What were the causes that led to the War of 1812, and what the results of the war?

8. Who made the first white settlement where the city of St. Louis now stands? New Orleans? Pittsburg? Great Salt Lake?

9. When did the Great Rebellion break out, and what was the first act of war?

10. Name some of the most important results of the war?

SET III.

TEN QUESTIONS—TEN CREDITS EACH.

1. Give an account of the settlement of Pennsylvania.

2. In what colony was religious liberty allowed?

3. To whom did the Mississippi Valley belong in 1754?

4. When was the last battle of the Revolution fought? What generals commanded the opposing forces?

5. When was the Federal Constitution formed, and when did it go into effect?

6. When, by whom, and where was Florida settled?

7. What territory did the United States acquire by purchase from France?

8. What connection had Texas with the Mexican War?

9. With what action, and when did the Great Rebellion begin; and with what, close?

10. What State was last admitted into the Union?

SET IV.

TEN QUESTIONS—TEN CREDITS EACH.

1. Mention the Colonial wars with the Indians.

2. Name five American generals in the Revolutionary War?

3. Name the leading events in 1777.

4. Who commanded the American army at the Battle of Bunker Hill, and when was that battle fought?

5. How long was the War of 1812?

6. What was the Boston Port Bill?

7. When was the tea thrown in Boston harbor, and what was the reason?

8. Name five naval engagements between the Americans and the British?

9. Who was the discoverer of North America?

10. Name the connection that the following names have with American history: De Soto; Sir Walter Raleigh; General Warren; General Putnam. S.

SET V.

TEN QUESTIONS—TEN CREDITS EACH.

1. Who made voyages of discovery to the New World before 1500?

2. When, where, and by people of what nation, was the first settlement made in Maryland? New York?

3. When, and for what purposes was the first union of the New England colonies formed? How long did that union last?

4. When, and where did the first Continental Congress meet, and what was done by it?

5. When was the battle of Long Island fought? Who was the American commander? the British commander? What was the result?

6. Who was Lafayette? Benedict Arnold?

7. What was the origin of the Constitution of the United States?

8. When, and from whom did the United States obtain Florida? Louisiana? California?

9. What was the cause of the great rebellion? What States passed ordinances of secession?

10. When was the battle of Gettysburg fought? Who were the commanders? What was the result? Where is Gettysburg?

UNITED STATES HISTORY.

SECOND GRADE.

SET I.

FIFTEEN QUESTIONS — FIVE CREDITS EACH.

1. FOR what events in the history of the Revolution is Philadelphia distinguished? New York?

2. For what events in the history of the Revolution is Boston distingished? Savannah?

3. When, where, and to whom did Lord Cornwallis surrender?

4. Name four battles in the Revolution in which the Americans were victorious; four in which they were defeated.

5. Where is Valley Forge, and for what event in the Revolution is it noted? Ticonderoga, and for what noted?

6. What was the Continental Congress, where did it meet, and who were its leading members?

7. Who were the most prominent men that took part in the Revolution, from the State of Virginia? Massachusetts? New York? Pennsylvania?

8. In what war was Quebec captured, and by whom?

9. In what war was Louisburg captured, and by whom?

10. In what war was Washington first engaged, and what was the most important expedition of that war?

11. What places in the present boundaries of the United States were originally settled by the Spanish? the French? the Dutch?

12. What were the two most important early Colonial settlements, and when and how were they made?

13. Name four Colonial wars, and one event in each.

14. Name an English, a Dutch, a Spanish, and an Italian discoverer.

15. Name four distinguished men connected with Colonial settlements; four distinguished generals of the American Revolution; two statesmen; one financier; one foreign minister; and one traitor of the Revolution. S.

GRAMMAR.

FIRST GRADE.

SET I.

TOTAL: SIXTEEN QUESTIONS — SIXTY CREDITS.

Ten Questions — Two Credits Each.

1. WRITE a complex interrogative sentence, and a compound declarative sentence.

2. Mention two ways of forming the plurals of nouns, and give examples.

3. Principal parts of the following verbs: *break*, *do*, *work*, *drink*, *bend*, *fly*.

4. What is meant by the rule: "A finite verb must agree with its subject in number and person."

5. Synopsis of the verb *go*, in the indicative mode, third person, singular number, interrogative form.

6. Conjugate the verb *go*, in the indicative mode, present tense, ancient form.

7. Write a sentence containing a relative pronoun, in the objective case, and tell what kind of a sentence it is.

8. Write a sentence containing the verb *sit* used in the future perfect, or second future tense: one containing the verb *lie*, in the past perfect tense.

9. Correct the following sentences, and give the reasons for correcting [no credits allowed unless the reasons are given]:—

My brother is older than me.

The people will not relinquish its rights.

10. Correct the following sentences, and give the reasons for correcting [no credits unless the reasons for correcting are given]: —

There was no boys at the party.

They thought it was me.

11. (6 *Credits.*) Correct the spelling, punctuation capitals, and grammatical errors, in the following paragraph: —

"But thou thyself moveth alone who can be a companyun of your course the oaks of the mountains falls the mountains theirselves decay with years the ocean shrink and grow again the Moon himself is lossed in Heaven but thou are forever the same rejoising in the briteness of thy coarse." — *Ossian.*

12. (2 *Credits.*) Write a list of the predicate verbs in the preceding paragraph, and place before each verb its appropriate subject.

13. (2 *Credits.*) How many principal clauses, or independent propositions, in the whole paragraph.

14. (*a.*) (2 *Credits.*) Correct and punctuate the following stanza: —

"the cricket chirps all day
"oh, farest summer stay"
the squirrel eyes askance the chestnuts browning
the wild-Fowl fly afar
above the foaming bar
and hasten southward ere the skies is frowning."

(*b.*) (2 *Credits.*) What kind of a sentence is this stanza, and why?

(*c.*) (2 *Credits.*) What is the object of *chirps*?

(*d.*) (2 *Credits.*) Parse *eyes.*

(*e.*) (2 *Credits.*) Parse *askance.*

15. "The years are heavy with weary sounds,
And their discord life's sweet music drowns."

(*a.*) (2 *Credits.*) What kind of a sentence is the preceding, and why?

(*b.*) (2 *Credits.*) Parse *drowns.*

(*c.*) (2 *Credits.*) Parse *music.*

(*d.*) (2 *Credits.*) Transpose the couplet into the order of a prose sentence.

(*e.*) (2 *Credits.*) Express the thoughts contained in these two lines in plain words, without figurative meaning.

16. Mr. and Mrs. Nutcracker were as respectable a pair of squirrels as ever wore gray brushes over their backs. "Depend upon it, my dear," said Mrs. Nutcracker, "that fellow must be a genius."

One Credit Each.

(*a.*) What kind of a sentence is the first?

(*b.*) What is the subject of *wore?*

(*c.*) In what case is *pair?*

(*d.*) What kind of a sentence is the second?

(*e.*) What is the subject of *depend?*

(*f.*) In what mode is *must be?*

(*g.*) Subject and predicate of the principal proposition in the second sentence.

(*h.*) What is the object of *said?*

(*i.*) Parse *that.*

(*j.*) Parse *genius.* S.

SET II.

TEN QUESTIONS—TEN CREDITS EACH.

1. What properties belong to verbs? Into what classes are verbs divided?

2. What properties belong to nouns, and into what classes are they divided?

3. Define a relative pronoun, and decline the pronouns *who* and *it.*"

4. How are adjectives compared?

5. Give a synopsis of the verb *love*, in the indicative mode, passive voice, third person, singular number, declarative form.

6. Write the plurals of the following nouns: *lady, money, pailful, cupful, memorandum.*

7. Parse each word in the following sentence "The Union must and shall be preserved."

8. Correct the following sentences: —

Them are the ones.
It is her.
She dresses very neat.
The rose smells sweetly.
Her dress looked splendidly.
I should not have went, if I had not expected to have received compensation.

1. Analyze the following sentence: "Education is the birthright of all."

10. Punctuate and correct the following: —

Mr brown Dear Sir i take my pen in hand to inform you that we are undergoing an examination and that if i survive I would like to have you call at 4 o'clock.

yours Truely. S.

SET III.

TEN QUESTIONS — TEN CREDITS EACH.

1. What are the essential properties of a noun?

2. Write the plural of *valley, folio, deer, wharf, spoonful, Mr., Miss, analysis, stratum.*

3. Compare *ill, less, round, bad, former, homely, pleasant.*

4. Name the principal parts of *lie, lay, sit, set, clothe, get, ride, sing*, and *run.*

5. What is the rule for the formation of a verb in the passive voice, and in the progressive form?

6. What is declension? conjugation?

7. Write a synopsis of the verbs *sing* and *swim*, in the indicative mode, third person, singular number.

8. Define a simple, a complex, and a compound sentence, and give an example of each.

9. In the sentence, "Let me teach you what is necessary," parse *let*, *what*, and *necessary*.

10. Correct the sentence, "I do not know who to send," and parse the relative pronoun. S.

SET IV.

TEN QUESTIONS—TEN CREDITS EACH.

1. Analyze the following sentence:—

"The completion of the Pacific Railroad was the occasion of great rejoicing in San Francisco and Chicago."

2. Parse *completion*, *occasion*, and *was*.

3. Decline the pronoun *her*; write the plural of *I*; plural of *radius*; compare *worst*, and decline *whom*.

4. What are the subordinate elements of a sentence?

5. Write a synopsis of the verb *eat*, in the indicative mode, third person, singular number.

6. Write a complex sentence and analyze it.

7. Write five rules for the use of capital letters.

8. In the sentence, "Let me go," parse each word.

9. Correct the following sentence, and give the reasons: "Between you and I, it was me who done it."

10. Conjugate the verb *write*, in the indicative mode, active voice, common form, future perfect tense.

SET V.

TEN QUESTIONS—TEN CREDITS EACH.

1. How many elementary sounds are there in the English language? Into what classes are they divided?

2. Define collective, abstract, and verbal nouns. Write examples.

3. Write the plurals of the following nouns: *fly*, *toy*, *wharf*, *roof*, *hero*, *folio*, *ox*, *son-in-law*, *pailful*, *a*, *3*, *scissors*, *dozen*, *radius*, and *stratum*.

4. Parse *him* and *what* in the sentence, "I gave him what he wanted."

5. Write a sentence containing the word *that* as a relative, an adjective, and a conjunction.

6. Write two sentences; the first containing a regular intransitive verb, and the second an irregular transitive verb.

7. Write the principal parts of the following verbs: *be*, *bid*, *bring*, *blow*, *choose*, *do*, *fly*, *give*, *lie* (to recline), *lay*, *see*, *sit*, *set*, *strive*, *swim*, *take*, *win*, *shoe*, *wear*, *weave*, and *write*, and give both forms when the verb has two.

8. Write a synopsis of the verb *ring*, in the third person singular of the indicative mode, active and passive voices.

9. Write a simple, a complex, and a compound sentence.

10. Correct the errors in the following sentences:

(*a*) Them are the ones.
(*b*) It is not me; it is her.
(*c*) A purse was lost in the street which contained a large sum of money.
(*d*) Horace, and I, and you are invited.
(*e*) The general, with all his soldiers, were taken.
(*f*) I seen him when he done it. S.

SET VI.

TEN QUESTIONS — TEN CREDITS EACH.

1. "Yes, it is I." Is *I* correctly used? Why, or why not?

2. What class of verbs govern two objective cases?

3. Analyze, "Whoever reads this, will be convinced."

4. Correct:—

> Whatever is is Right this world tis true
> Was made for caesar but for Titus too.

5. Parse *servant* and *go* in the following: "He bade the servant go."

6. Give five forms of expressing the idea, "A wolf let into the sheep-fold will devour the sheep."

7. What is the rule for the use of *shall* and *will?*

8. Give the case of *horse* in each sentence, and the rule:—

> The *horse* running away, the wagon was overturnéd.
> The horse, running away, overturned the wagon.

9. Describe a primitive, also a derivative word, and give examples of each.

10. Correct and give reasons:—

> Who did you see? It certainly could not have been me.
> Who broke this pitcher? Not her; it was me.
> Who is that boy speaking to?

SET VII.

TWELVE QUESTIONS — FIVE CREDITS EACH.

1. What is a relative pronoun?

2. Name the properties belonging to a verb.

3. Give the rule for forming the possessive singular; also the possessive plural of nouns. How do you form the possessive of pronouns?

4. Give the plural of *beef, alkali, cuckoo, portico,* 8, *Mr., man-servant, this, penny, gold.*

5. Give the rule for forming the comparison regularly. Compare *good, black, little, old, ill.*

6. Tell how a verb is conjugated in the passive voice.

7. Write a synopsis of the verb *row*, in the first person singular, in the indicative and potential modes, and in the progressive and interrogative forms combined.

8 Write the principal parts of the verbs, *sing*, *go*, *do*, *eat*, *swim*, *ought*, *lay*, *shall*, *work*.

9. What auxiliary verbs must always be used in the present perfect tense, the future perfect tense, and the past perfect tense?

10. Analyze the following sentence: "The evil *which men do live* after *them*. Also, parse the words italicized.

11. Write the following sentences correctly:—

(*a*) The eldest of the two sons is going to school.

(*b*) Give me them books.

(*c*) Spelling is easier than to read or write.

(*d*) Some discussion arose in regard to whom should be sent.

(*e*) John, he went, but the rest, they all stayed at home.

12. Give the following rules in spelling:—

(*a*) For doubling the final consonant.

(*b*) For dropping *e*.

GRAMMAR.

SECOND GRADE.

SET I.

TEN QUESTIONS—TEN CREDITS EACH.

1. DECLINE *her*, *us*, and *who*.

2. Conjugate the verb *be* in the indicative mood, future perfect tense.

3. Write a simple sentence containing only an adjective, a noun, an object, and an adverb, and parse each word.

4. In what different ways is the plural of nouns formed.

5. Analyze the sentence, "Let me go," and parse each word.

6. Give five directions for the use of capital letters.

7. Write a sentence containing a verb in the progressive form, one containing an infinitive used as the subject of a verb, and one containing a verb in the passive voice.

8. Analyze the sentence, "I told him when to go," and parse *told* and *to go*.

9. Give the principal parts of the following verbs: *burst*, *dig*, *shoot*, *tear*, *go*, *lie*, *sit*, *flee*, *fly*, and *teach*.

10. Define *subject*, *predicate*, *phrase*, and *clause*.

S.

SET II.

TWENTY QUESTIONS — FIVE CREDITS EACH.

1. What is a collective noun? Give three examples.
2. How do nouns ending in *y* form their plurals?
3. What classes of nouns have no plural?
4. Define nominative case.
5. What is meant by *object* as used in grammar?
6. How is the possessive case plural of nouns formed?
7. Write the possessive case singular and plural of *city* and *life*.
8. What is a compound pronoun? How many classes?
9. How are compound personal pronouns formed?
10. Write a sentence containing the relative *which* in the possessive case.
11. How many general methods of comparison?
12. Compare *this, discreet, blue, meagre, supreme.*
13. What is an irregular verb? Give an example.
14. What is the natural order of the elements of an English sentence?
15. What is the principal mode?
16. What is the difference between *conjugation* and *synopsis*?
17. Name the defective verbs?
18. How is a verb conjugated in the passive voice?
19. What is the difference between primitive and lerivative words?
20. Write a good definition of a verb.

SET III.

FIFTEEN QUESTIONS—FIVE CREDITS EACH.

1. What is the authority which decides whether any sentence is grammatical or not?

2. Give the ordinary grammatical classification of words.

3. Give ten forms of the personal pronoun.

4. Define transitive and intransitive verbs, and give an example of each in separate sentences.

5. "Water is froze easier than alcohol." Correct this sentence, and give the reasons for correction.

6. How do you form the plural of nouns?

7. How do you form the possessives of plural nouns?

8. What is a relative pronoun? Decline *who.*

9. When is *that* to be substituted for *who* or *which*?

10. Write a sentence containing the verb *to do*, in the indicative mode, third past tense, third person, plural number, passive voice.

11. Give the verb *to be*, in the first person, singular number, in all the tenses of the indicative mode.

12. What do you mean by emphatic, and interrogative forms?

13. Give the principal parts of *burst, dare, lie, lay,* and *slay.*

14. What are expletives?

15. Write three sentences, using *but* as a conjunction in the first, as an adverb in the second, and as a preposition in the third.

GRAMMAR.

THIRD GRADE.

SET I.

TWENTY QUESTIONS — THREE CREDITS EACH.

1. Name and define the two leading parts of speech.
2. Write and analyze a simple sentence.
3. Define a personal pronoun : a conjunction.
4. Decline the pronouns *me* and *her*.
5. Compare *little* and *more*.
6. Write a sentence containing an adjective, a noun, a verb, and an adverb.
7. Analyze it.
8. Parse each word.
9. Give a synopsis of the verb *be* or *am* in the indicative mode, first person.
10. Conjugate the verb *be* in the past tense.
11. Name two ways in which the plural of nouns is formed, and give examples.
12. Form the possessive plural of *woman*; of the pronoun *he*.
13. Compare *good, more, skillful, ready*.
14. Write a compound sentence.
15. Synopsis of the verb *love* in the indicative mode, third person, singular number.
16. Principal parts of *do, go, write, shine*.
17. Write a sentence containing a transitive verb.

18. Write a sentence containing a verb in the passive voice.

19. When is the artice *an* used instead of *a*.

20. Analyze the sentence: "Pupils who study will improve."

21. (5 *Credits.*) Correct the spelling, punctuation, capitals, and the grammatical errors of the following paragraph:—

"George jones was a idle boy he did not love to study the teacher of the schule offen told him if he did not study diligently when young he would never succede well george wood ofen go to skool without haveing maid any prepparasion for his mourning lessun and when called to resite he would make so menny blunders that the rest of the class could not help laffing at him."

22. (5 *Credits.*) Write a list of all the nouns in the preceding sentence.

23. (5 *Credits.*) Write a list of all the verbs.

24. (5 *Credits.*) Write a list of all the adjectives.

25. (5 *Credits.*) Correct the following stanza of poetry:—

THE CAMMEL.

"Cammel thou are good and mild
dosile as a little child
thou was made for usefulness
men to comfort and to bless
thou doth clothe him thou do feed
thou does lend to him your speed."

26. (5 *Credits.*) Change the preceding stanza into a paragraph of prose. S.

SET II.

TEN QUESTIONS — TEN CREDITS EACH.

1. Write a correct sentence containing *which* as a relative pronoun.

2. Name the objective case, singular and plural, of each of the plural pronouns.

3. Write a sentence containing an interrogative pronoun in the objective case.

4. Conjugate the verb *to go* in the imperfect tense, indicative mood.

5. Give the subject of the following sentence: "The good little boy obeys his parents."

6. Correct the sentence, "It was me who rode the horse."

7. Change the verb in the following sentence into the perfect tense: "Were you in Chicago?"

8. Write a sentence containing the word *order* used as a noun, also a sentence in which it is used as a verb.

9. "If Cæsar was ambitious, he was at the same time magnanimous." Give the parts of speech in the above sentence.

10. Write a sentence containing the verb *obey* in the passive voice and future tense,

SET III.

TEN QUESTIONS—TEN CREDITS EACH.

1. Write the possessive case, plural number of *man, woman.*

2. Give the case of each pronoun in the sentence: "She went with us to her house."

3. Name the subject, predicate, and object in the following sentence: "The industrious boy studied his lesson diligently."

4. Correct: "He gave them apples to you and I."

5. Write a sentence containing an adjective in the superlative degree, and a noun in the possessive case, plural number.

6. Write a sentence containing the comparative of *ill.*

7. "Henry asked his father his sister's age." Name the case of each noun.

8. Write a sentence using two adverbs derived from adjectives, and underline them.

9. Correct: "He done it very good."

10. In the sentence, "John played a game of marbles," change the verb to the passive voice.

SET IV.

TEN QUESTIONS — TEN CREDITS EACH.

1. Define a pronoun.

2. Name the properties of nouns and pronouns.

3. Name five interjections.

4. Decline *her.*

5. Correct the following sentence: "Mary gave the two oranges to Jane and I."

6. Compare the following adjectives: *square, ill.*

7. Name the properties of the verb.

8. Give the plural of *ox*, *knife*, *miss*, *child*, and the letter *s*.

9. "He is a scholar," parse *scholar.*

10. Write a sentence contaning a transitive verb and its object.

11. Write the feminine of the following: *Uncle*, *man*, *son*, *lad*, and *lord.*

12. In the sentence, "Charles, bring me a book," parse *Charles.*

13. How are the comparative and superlative degree formed?

14. Write the possessive plural of *woman.*

15. Give the second future tense of the verb *write* in both numbers.

SET V.

TEN QUESTIONS — TEN CREDITS EACH.

1. What parts of speech are compared? What conjugated?

2. Compare *benevolent* in two ways.

3. Synopsis of the verb *to write* in indicative mood, third person, singular number.

4. Name the properties belonging to nouns; properties belonging to verbs.

5. Write appropriate connectives in place of the dashes in the following sentences: —

—— you are weary, you may rest.
I do not believe —— he will go.
—— he desert me, I will trust him.

6. Correct the following sentences: —

I told him to set down, and he laid down.
I seen the coat before he had wore it.

7. Fill the following blanks with plural nouns: —

The —— are very beautiful.
Time will set all —— right
James and his —— were here.
I have seen the —— with their ——.

8. Compare the adverbs *badly, far, much, well.*

9. Decline the nouns *man, wife.*

10. Write this sentence and correct misspelled words: —

The potatos roted upon the prarie and the monkies ate up the caulliflowers, while the tomatoes were troden down by the couragous annimals which were destitute of principal.

SET VI.

TEN QUESTIONS — THREE CREDITS EACH.

1. What is a verb?

2. What is the subject of a sentence? The predicate?

3. What properties have nouns?

4. When is a verb in the passive voice?

5. What is meant by the person and number of verbs?

6. What is a phrase?

7. What is a personal pronoun?

8. How are verbs divided with reference to their terminations?

9. What is the masculine of *miss?* Of *bride?* The feminine of *lad?*

10. Write the plurals of *story, piano, shelf, she, I, penny, synopsis, gold, swine.*

Ten Questions — Four Credits Each.

11. Decline the pronoun *me, which.*

12. Write the principal parts of the following verbs: *bid, sing, run, ride.*

13. Write a synopsis of the verb *be,* in the indicative mode.

14. Conjugate the verb *write* in the indicative mode, active voice, future perfect tense.

15. Synopsis of the verb *row* in the potential mode, passive voice.

16. Write the verb *study* in the progressive form, indicative mode, past perfect tense, third person, singular number; in the negative form, present perfect tense.

17. How is the passive voice of transitive verbs formed?

18. Conjugate the verb *be* in the infinitive mode.

19. Compose a sentence containing a subject, predicate, object, adjective, and adverb.

20. Write a sentence in which a phrase is used as the subject.

Five Questions — Six Credits Each.

21. Write a sentence having a clause for its subject.

22. Write a sentence having a collective noun; one having a compound relative pronoun.

23. Write a sentence to illustrate the emphatic form of the verb, and the ancient or solemn style of the verb.

24. Write a sentence containing only a subject, predicate, and object, and parse each word.

25. What rules can you give for the use of capital letters and periods? S.

GRAMMAR.

FOURTH GRADE.

SET I.

FIFTEEN QUESTIONS — THREE CREDITS EACH.

1. A *name* is what?

2. The word or phrase which shows what we talk about is what?

3. The word which tells what a thing *is*, what it *does*, or what is done to it, is what?

4. In the following sentences draw *one* line under each noun and *two* lines under each verb:

Ella dreaded examination.
A path through woods.
He reached eighty per cent.
She waved her golden hair.

5. To express an actual occurrence or fact we use what mood?

6. "You *must* succeed." In what mode is *must*?

7. "I did it *myself*." What is *myself*?

8. Write the principal parts of the verbs *go*, *sing*, *drink*.

9. What kind of a verb does not have a nominative?

10. What kind of a verb has no object?

11. Write the verb *read* in the active voice, indicative mode, present tense, singular number, first person.

12. Examinations may seem hard, but they do us much good. What is *but?*

13. "I don't know nothing about it." Correct that sentence. Tell why.

14. What is that form of the verb which always ends in *ing?*

15. What kind of a noun distinguishes one particular thing from all others of the same kind?

SET II.

TEN QUESTIONS — TEN CREDITS EACH.

1. Write an affirmative sentence and change it to a negative.

2. Correct "Me and him went after them boys."

3. Point out the nouns in the following sentence, and give their number: "The little girl had some apples in her satchel."

4. Change the nouns in this sentence to the singular: "Those children are writing on their slates."

5. Write a sentence containing a noun in the possessive case.

6. "I know whose book that is." What case is *whose?*

7. Write the plurals of *mouse, fly, goose, ox,* and *bird.*

8. Write an interrogative sentence.

9. Pick out the name-words: *Sea, see, scene, seen, lane, lain, road, rode, clothes, close.*

10. Write a sentence containing an adjective in the superlative degree.

SET III.

TEN QUESTIONS — TEN CREDITS EACH.

1. "Men dig rocks and metals out of the earth." Name the nouns.

2. What two adjectives have plurals?

3. Correct this sentence: "Them apples has a stem."

4. Write a sentence with a quality-word in it.

5. Write a sentence having two action-words in it.

6. Make this sentence mean more than one: "This man is very tall."

7. Point out the quality-words in the following: "The nice little girl lost her new white apron."

8. "Henry played in the shade. James worked hard." Which of the two action-words denotes present time?

9. Give the plurals of these words: *Man, woman, foot, thief, lady.*

10. Change to singular: "These women sew, and those men work."

NATURAL PHILOSOPHY.

FIRST GRADE.

SET I.

FIFTEEN QUESTIONS — FIVE CREDITS EACH.

1. WHAT do you mean when you say that a body weighs an ounce?

2. What is uniform motion?

3. How will a body move when acted upon by forces that operate in different directions?

4. How is a clock regulated?

5. What is reaction?

6. What is the line of direction of a body?

7. How is the pressure of fluids exerted?

8. How may the specific gravity of bodies that will sink in water be ascertained?

9. What causes sounds to be louder or fainter?

10. How does moisture in the air affect the transmission of sound?

11. Why is a linen garment cool?

12. What is the angle of vision?

13. When does refraction of light take place?

14. What is lightning?

15. What is light?

SET II.

TEN QUESTIONS — TEN CREDITS EACH.

1. What is physics?

2. On what principle does the method of determining specific gravity depend?

3. A body weighs one pound in the air ; one pound of iron being attached, it just sinks. What is its specific gravity ?

4. An inclined plane is one foot high and sixteen feet long. What force will be required to raise one pound upon it ?

5. Mention two laws of falling bodies.

6. A body is thrown upwards from the surface of the earth with a velocity of 64⅓ feet per second ; how high will it rise ?

7. What substances are most sonorous ?

8. What substances are the best conductors of heat ?

9. What is polarized light ?

10. What distinguishes statical from dynamical electricity ?

SET III.

1. How many forces will act upon a body thrown horizontally ?

2. On what does the time occupied in the vibration of a pendulum depend ?

3. How is the upward pressure of a fluid shown ?

4. For what is a barometer used ?

5. How does moisture in the air affect the velocity of sound ?

6. Why is a linen garment cool ?

7. When you look into a plane mirror, where will your image appear to be ?

8. What effect is produced by light passing through a convex lens ?

9. What is the Leyden jar ?

10. How can an artificial magnet be made ?

SET IV.

1. What is the law of attraction of gravitation?
2. What is meant by "specific gravity?"
3. What are the laws which govern the refraction of light?
4. What is the barometer, and who invented it?
5. Name the mechanical powers.
6. How are waves caused?
7. What is the velocity of sound?
8. What are the principal effects of heat?
9. On what does the color of bodies depend?
10. What planets are exterior to the orbit of the earth?
11. What is the ecliptic?
12. How is the change of seasons caused?
13. What is the galaxy?
14. What causes the tides?
15. What causes an eclipse of the sun? S.

BOOK-KEEPING.

SET I.

1. PREPARE day-book, cash-book, and ledger forms.

2. Enter the following transactions in the proper books :—

SAN FRANCISCO, *April* 10, 1870.

Sold J. Forward, on account, 10 lbs. coffee @ 20 cts. ; 15 lbs. brown sugar @ 15 cts. Paid for drayage, $2.50. Received of J. Forward, $2.00 on account.

3. Write a receipt for $100.

4. Write a promissory note for $500, interest 1¼ per cent. per month ; date, to-day, with indorsement.

5. Make out a bill of the following items :—

SAN FRANCISCO, *April* 10, 1870.

S. Jones bought of John Worth, 10 lbs. tea @ 80 cts. ; 9 lbs. China rice, @ 5 cts. ; 20 lbs. crushed sugar, @ 14 cts. ; 10 lbs. butter, @ 40 cts.

Receipt the bill.

SET II.

1. What is book-keeping ?

2. Define the double-entry system.

3. What besides personal accounts are kept in double-entry ledger ?

4. What should be the character of the day-book ?

5. What is an account ?

6. Into what classes may accounts be divided?

7. State the principles for debiting and crediting the various accounts.

8. When an account is closed, how is shown the balance or difference?

9. How are resources, liabilities, losses, and gains shown in the ledger?

10. State the six steps in closing the ledger.

11. Post the following and close the ledger:—

	Dr.	Cr.		Dr.	Cr.
Stock	$600	$2,800	Expense	$75	
Merchandise . . .	3,470	2,400	Cash	1,600	$925
Bills receivable . .	2,750	1,800	Wm. Brown. . . .	180	270
Bills payable . . .	240	1,200	Jas. Campbell. . .	900	420

Inventory, $1,250.

12. Write a promissory note for $500, sixty days, and indorse in full.

13. Write a sight draft for $100, and accept.

14. Write a bank check for $200.

15. Write a receipt in full for $75.

SET III.

TEN QUESTIONS — FIVE CREDITS EACH.

1. What is the purpose of the art of book-keeping?

2. Write a promissory note.

3. January 12, 1868, Doe bought of Roe 225 lbs. of sugar at $0.08 per pound. Write out the bill which Roe should render to Doe.

4. Rule a day-book page.

5. Rule a ledger page.

6. Rule a cash-book page.

7. Write out the entry which Doe should make in his day-book.

8. Write out the entry which Roe should make in his ledger.

9. February 4, 1868, Doe paid Roe in full for the sugar. Write out the entry which Roe should make in his cash-book.

10. Write out the receipt given by Roe to Doe.

CPSIA information can be obtained
at www.ICGtesting.com
Printed in the USA
LVHW112020030423
743357LV00006B/654